Fall From Apocalypse
2nd Edition
By
J. Wayne Frye

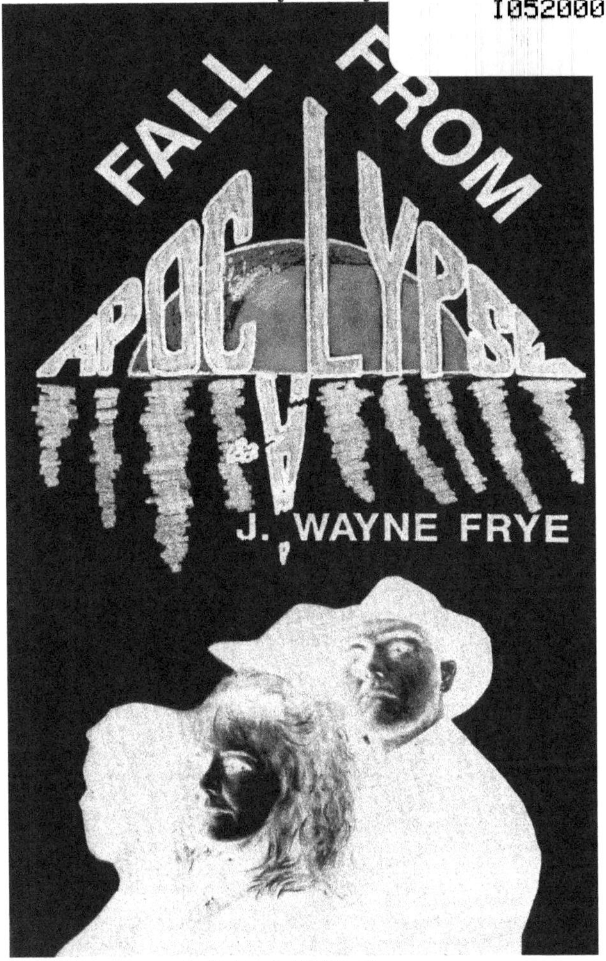

I0520002

Original 1993 Cover

Fall From Apocalypse

The Author

Wayne Frye's Aaron Adams series has been popular among Canadian mystery lovers since first appearing in 2005. He provides satirical political commentary to many Canadian newspapers, and his books on politics have created a great deal of controversy. He has written marketing/advertising textbooks, been a successful U.S. university hockey coach, professor, university President and served as a marketing consultant to hockey teams and entertainment companies. He has been cited for his work with inner-city gang children in the Los Angeles area and been active in the anti-globalization movement. He became a Canadian citizen in 2003 and lives with his wife in Ladysmith, British Columbia.

Other Books by J. Wayne Frye

The Fall From Apocalypse
Armageddon Now
Worth
Hockey Mania and the Mystery of Nancy Running Elk
When Jesus Came to Jersey as the Son of Thunder
Something Evil in the Darkness at Hopkins House
How Hockey Saved a Jew From the Holocaust:
The Rudi Ball Story
The Catastrophic Calamities of a Village Idiot
Fighting for Justice in the Land of Hypocrisy
Guide to Alternative Education (13 Editions)
Cataclysmic Dreams in Black and White
Mastering Marketing Research
Introduction to Advertising
Marketing Plan Work Book
Public Relations Workbook
Promotions Workbook
Advertising Design

Books by J. Wayne Frye with Jasmine H. Frye

Canadian Angels of Mercy – Nurses in Times of Peril
Points of Rebellion: North American Aboriginals
Who Fought for Justice

(Most of the above available from amazon.com)

J. Wayne Frye

The Aaron Adams books have been a favourite of Canadian mystery lovers since 2005. Now, Wayne Frye has up-dated his original 1993 USA novel that introduced this magnificent defender of the downtrodden. Finally, we will be taken back to the very beginning and see how it all started in 1969.

FROM THE BOOK

In the beginning there was sanity, only in small doses, but sanity nevertheless. As time passed, a nation's mind deteriorated into a mere shell of its former self, until finally, all the years of dreams, hopes and promises flowed into a river of mediocrity that emptied into a vast dark pit of nothingness.

I was not intimidated by anybody who thought they were powerful, because I lived to make the powerful realize that there was still someone left who had no fear in a world filled with sheep who cowered in supplication to those who thought they were to be exalted because of the position they held. Government bureaucrat, politician, minister, business tycoon, royalty – they were all leeches in my book, living off the labour of the working man. I had no respect for any of them.

Williams took one look at that big bastard of a forty-five. One look was all he had time for.

DEDICATION - 2012 EDITION
A NOTE OF THANKS
TO MY MILITARY COMRADES
WITH WHOM I SHARED
A SOJOURN IN HELL

Writing prose attacking the Vietnam War and the ills of America was a great release for my frustration at a time when I was overwhelmed with melancholy for being a part of an organization I deplored. Therefore, to those with whom I shared the aforementioned prose, I want to include a brief note of thanks to my fellow U.S. Army Field Detachment "O" comrades who, along with me, endured the wretchedness of serving at a time when conscription gave us no choice, other than desertion or jail, but to take part in an ill-advised, immoral and totally unnecessary war. To William, Marshall, Howard, Steve, Lorne, Randy, Ron, Bill, Frank, Charlie, Noble, Tom, Emily, Suzanne, Jenny and the many others whose names have faded into the recesses of an aging mind, a simple thanks to all of you for sharing my youth and making my time in hell bearable. How ironic that we could actually have fun and share an unforgettable camaraderie in all that misery.

DEDICATED TO: My mother, who always loved a good mystery, and to my dad, who always loved my mother. (Original dedication 1993.)

J. Wayne Frye

Fall From Apocalypse

TABLE OF CONTENTS

Fall From Apocalypse

2nd Edition
Copyright 2012 in Canada
by
J. Wayne Frye
Original USA Copyright 1993
by
J. Wayne Frye

Catalogue Number: 20126196110

ISBN: 87527-520-6 (1993) - USA
978-0-9879728-3-5 (2012)- Canada
Peninsula Publishing

Fireside Books – Victoria, British Columbia
Originally published by Warren H. Green, Inc.

J. Wayne Frye

Fall From Apocalypse

PROLOGUE
THE HORSEMAN WAS AARON ADAMS

In the beginning there was sanity, only in small doses, but sanity nevertheless. As time passed, a nation's mind deteriorated into a mere shell of its former self, until finally, all the years of dreams, hopes and promises flowed into a raging river of mediocrity that emptied into a vast, dark pit of nothingness.

In this cruel, inhuman, warmongering system of ineptitude and ignorance walked one of the four horsemen of the Apocalypse. He was a man not quite as human as you and I, but he was capable of loving, although he was much better at hating, hating all those who crassly and unabashedly exploited the masses for personal gain.

This hate swelled up into a fury of murder and mayhem, barely skirting legality, so the horseman might survive to kill again. It was his destiny to destroy those who practiced deception and enslaved the poor and downtrodden to a bankrupt idea of salvation offered by an economic system that promoted greed as an enviable trait.

Though buoyed upward by a single ray of love, this demon of the darkness struck fear into the hearts of those who preyed on the masses. Fear that the horseman would come calling, shielded and protected by the darkness that engulfs us all.

Through the years, the horseman was unaware of his role, as many of us are unaware of ours. But one single event in his life made him fall from Apocalypse, fall into the pangs of hell.

Gripped by pain and despair, he meandered through the corridors of fire, aimlessly wandering in the kingdom of darkness, until he scaled the walls of hopelessness to stand once again upon Apocalypse, astride the palest of the four horses. The horse was death and the horseman was Aaron Adams.

CHAPTER I
I HAD A REAL DILLY IN MIND

Williams took one look at that big bastard of a forty-five. One look was all he had time for. The son-of-a-bitch hit the payment with a resounding thud. I looked down at him and let out a satisfied grin, the one with all the teeth showing. I smiled so long and so hard that my jaws ached.

Damn, it felt good to stand over the bastard and watch his eyes roll back in his head while blood oozed out of the big hole in his chest. The son-of-bitch thought he would get me. What a laugh that was. Williams wasn't laughing. His eyes were pleading for mercy where there was none. Hell was waiting for him, and I was prepared to dispatch him there post-haste, and if any more of his kind got in my way, hell would be more crowded than the Los Angeles Freeway at rush hour.

Blood streamed out of the side of his mouth in slow trickles. Damn, he looked too peaceful lying there on the pavement, breathing like a long distance runner who had just finished a race. I walked over, looked down at the bastard and grinned as he looked up at me pleading for mercy. Mercy hell. I put my left foot in his half-open mouth and cursed as his crumbling teeth scratched my new shoes. Damn, I was going to enjoy taking my foot out. I brought the left side of his jaw out with it. What the hell, he didn't need a jaw where he was going.

Too bad the son-of-bitch had to pass-out. He missed the best part of the show. I never like his looks, besides, in hell he wouldn't need a face. I stomped hell out of it. When I finished that little chore, I made mince meat out of what was left. Damn, my feet were sore.

I picked up his overcoat, scraped up what was left of the bastard with it and dumped him in the trashcan. He was home now.

Damn, I felt good. Another two-bit, gun-toting, strong-arm bastard was off the streets courtesy of Aaron Adams.

She was waiting for me, just like always. A big smile crept across her face as I walked toward her.

She said in her low, sultry voice that seemed to vibrate with sexuality, "hi tiger, you look as if you have been on the prowl."

I pulled off my jacket, untied my shoulder strap and gave her a slap on the ass, as I pulled her to me for a warm embrace.

"This tiger is tired baby, real tired. I left one of the syndicate's boys in a trash can off 43rd. The bastards still have a contract out on me, but they will have a hard time finding another taker after Fluke Dodd's sordid picture hits the scandal sheets. They couldn't bury what is left of him in a kid's sand box."

"You're not hurt Aaron?"

"Have I ever been? I am a wrecking machine."

"You're body is a mass of scars."

"Just scratches, doll, mere scratches. Besides, your body is not flawless. You never have told me how you got that scar on that beautiful shapely butt of yours."

Winking at Aaron, she replied, "I never will either baby. My butt is my own business."

Aaron, smiling broadly, replied, "not when I am around. Then it is my business, the same as the rest of your body, and I may just hop in bed with you any minute, now."

Damn, what a woman, B.J. Holton. She was about 5:9, 135 pounds and neatly stacked into a voluptuous 38-25-38 frame of explosive TNT. And to top it off, she had a ticket, a ticket that made her a lethal weapon on the streets of New York, ready to do battle – B.J. Holton, private eye.

Fall From Apocalypse

She had come to me over two years ago, looking for a job. Hell, I couldn't even afford a full-time secretary, so what the hell, I took on a full time partner, and what a partner she was. The sign on the door still read Adams Investigations, but her poise and charm had brought in a deluge of clients. Clients who might have looked elsewhere, if it were not for her sexy smile, lithe body and down-right uncanny ability to bring in more business than we could handle.

I had done alright before, made a living anyway, but since she graced the place with her looks and talent. the dough kept rolling in too fast to count. Of course, the headlines I frequently made hadn't hurt business either.

Still, she was a mystery. She was a stranger, although I had known her for two years. She admitted to being 26 years old, but offered no references when she walked into my office in 1967, seeking a job. Through my own nosing around, I had discovered she had worked as a go-go dancer in night clubs up and down the strip for three or four years, but there was a big gap between her twenty-first birthday and the day she came to work for me. It was a gap even a crack private-eye like me had been unable to fill. She insisted on not talking about it, so I just assumed it involved some disastrous love-affair that was best forgotten. After all, no matter what I found out, she would still be a mystery to me.

Fall From Apocalypse

What puzzled me most was how she could fall for a guy like me. Aaron Adams, the tough guy on the east-side, who wasn't worth her time. I had seen and done it all and my looks showed it. I wasn't built too badly – 6:3, about 210, but that is where it ended. My face showed much more than my 37 years – much more. The brown eyes carried heavy baggage from too many fights, too much booze and not enough sleep. The face was laced with scars from years of barroom brawling, and the nose had that customary bend from being broken one time too many. All the teeth were still there, but not hinged up as tightly as they used to be. I wasn't ready for the freak show, but I was certainly a long way from being a Paul Newman. Hell, I had a way to go before I could catch Bogart.

I stood there with my arms wrapped around the nearest thing to heaven a man could ask for. It was a mystery, but it was a mystery I wasn't interested in solving. I planted a long passionate kiss on her moist lips and began to ease her toward the sofa, when she dug in her feet into the floor and brought me to a screeching halt.

"Slow down, tiger, slow down. You still have work to do tonight."

"Yeah, I know, and you are interrupting it." I said as I squeezed my arms tightly around her slender waist and began to nibble on her ear.

"Whoa tiger, a guy named Bill Lawrence came by to see you earlier tonight. Said it was really important that he see you right away."

"Hell, Bill can wait. He is just an old army buddy."

B.J. , a bit perturbed, replied, "maybe, but he said he wanted you to help an old buddy in trouble."

Now, I was perturbed. I said, "hell, I am interested in helping myself right now. You could make things a little easier."

Smiling, B.J. gave me that coy look. "That would take all the fun out of it."

Then she gave me that mischievous wink and said, "besides, when somebody gives you a $500 retainer, and a box of smuggled Cuban cigars from that dirty commie, Castro, whom we are all taught to hate by our all-knowing government, perhaps you should get to work."

"Bill gave you $500 as a retainer? Hell, he is a friend."

"Yeah, I told him that it wasn't necessary until you talked to him, but he said that if Paul needed your help as much as he thought he did, you'd earn that and plenty more."

Fall From Apocalypse

Letting go of her, I backed up a bit and gave her a quizzical look. "You mean Paul Cross?"

"That's the name he gave me, tiger."

I made a quick about face, put on my rod, and gave B.J. a kiss on the forehead, as I buttoned up my coat. "Paul's close baby, real close. I'll check it out and be back in an hour or so."

"Check, tiger."

I walked out of the office, banged the elevator button until my hand was sore, then gave-up and walked down the eight flights of stairs like I always did. Damn elevator never worked.

The chill outside began to creep into my bones, as I walked block after block in search of a taxi. Hell, I should have driven myself, but my car was in the garage for repair, and B.J. never drove her car to work on Wednesdays. She let her landlady use it. Hell she was always doing somebody a favour. I began to wonder if she would do me a favour when I got back. I had a real dilly in mind.

CHAPTER 2
GOODNIGHT BOYS

Why did the few make life so miserable for the many? Why couldn't a decent citizen walk the streets at night without fear of harm? Could it be because the few made it impossible for the many to survive in a land dedicated to worshipping at the feet of those with power and riches? How could the average person survive without resorting to outright thievery? If you robbed a convenience store, it was a crime, but if you represented Wall Street or the banks, robbery was just business.

Not everyone could have the privilege of living in modern day castles in gated communities, protected and walled off from the rest of society that was not worthy of the so-called good things in life. The wealthy were to be worshipped and feared by a society that let all good things flow to those at the top.

Strolling through the Bowery, I felt the ill wind of despair. Looking at the poor remnants of human beings lying in the doorways and alleys who had been discarded in service to greed, I asked myself what prospects did city life hold except the promise of graft and fear. This was the price paid so that the few could lounge in luxury while the rest of us struggled for a bone from the table of plenty.

Fall From Apocalypse

Damn, I needed a cab. Even taxi drivers did not like coming to this part of the city. Anyway, how many people in the bowery could afford even a short cab ride, especially since the small operators were all being squeezed out by the two corporate behemoth cab companies that had the politicians in their pockets, so they could control the number of cab licences handed out.

Meanwhile, you would have no problem finding a cab uptown in the theatre district, where the rich walked out of over-priced stage productions in lavish theatres designed to accommodate the high and mighty. The taxis lined up to accommodate the rich while the rest of us strolling the streets had the pleasure of gazing upon the privileged class. I never ceased to be amazed at how the underprivileged lined up to worship the privileged, as if they were Gods. I remembered how the streets had been lined a few years earlier with the poor who cheered as the British queen's motorcade sped down Broadway. Why do people grovel and beg to worship the parasitic morons who think just by birth they are better than the rest of us? What was it that old philosopher once said – *men line up to be made slaves*. Hell, even revolutions that were supposed to help the poor usually wound up with a select few on top. Then, you had the USA to contend with, as it was fearful of any system that might not be capitalistic in nature. Just ask Che and Fidel what it was like to stand up to the

United States. You either did it America's way or you paid a heavy price.

What the hell, I would never solve the problems of the world. The rich would always be rich, and the poor were too stupid to do anything about it. I had to worry about Paul Cross. What the hell was going on? The son-of-bitch seemed to be loaded. He was immaculately dressed and manicured the last time I saw him. We had seen trouble together, big trouble in a big war. All wars were big when you were the one dodging the bullets. While the rich and connected got draft deferments, the poor folks had to fight.

Paul and I had never really kept in touch, but ran into each other on occasion by chance. It had been eight or nine months since I had seen him. I knew his address, but had never visited before. The address was on Lorton Street in lower Manhattan. I knew it was near the Bowery, but never really considered that he was living in the ghetto. As I turned down 43rd, a cab finally appeared out of the fog. I gave a loud whistle and the driver slammed on his brakes so hard, smoke came out of the wheel well. I walked over, opened the back door and got in.

As I closed the door, the driver turned his head, smiled through rotted teeth and said, "where to, man?"

Fall From Apocalypse

"Lorton Street."

Shaking his head vigorously, he replied, "hell man, you don't want to go down miserable place after dark. That place is the real arm-pit of Manhattan."

"That's funny, I have never been there. Haven't ever heard of it."

"Yeah, and you don't want to go, believe me. If you are going for the cheap pussy, believe me, it ain't worth it. I got a sister who gets checked weekly, and she will do you real good for a ten spot. She really knows the ropes. She'll do it all. Even knows how to use a whip, if you like that sort of thing. But man, them women on Lorton Street will give you the rots. Lots of guys go down there for the cheap stuff, but two or three dollars ain't much of a bargain when your pecker starts oozing pus.

A little disgusted, I gave him the piercing eyes and frowned slow and hard. "You're full of knowledge buddy, but I'm not after a woman. All I want to do is make a social call."

"It's your money, Jack," he replied.

As he sped away in the dense fog, I said, "right man, it is my money. 1435 Lorton and hurry. I am pressed for time."

About five minutes later, we pulled up in front of a dingy 10 or 11 story brownstone building that looked like it had lost a ferocious battle with a wrecking ball, but still managed to precariously stand to serve those who were ignored by a society more interested in serving the rich than showing compassion for the downtrodden. A couple of tough-looking hoods with cigarettes dangling from their lips stood defiantly in the doorway of the building, as if they were knights guarding a castle.

Leaning forward, I told the cabby to stick around, because I wouldn't be long. He replied, "sorry man, it ain't healthy to sit in a parked car around here. I'll have to pass. Give the company a call when you get ready to leave and ask for me, number 814."

I handed him five dollars, told him to keep the change and said, "never mind waiting, I will walk."

Shaking his head furiously, he let out a sigh as he said, "man, you're asking for it," and then floored it and smoke came out of the wheel well again, as he streaked down the street.

The two hoods stepped out of the doorway and ambled my way with arrogant, cocky strides that were contrived to instil fear in those who might stand up to them.

Fall From Apocalypse

The tallest one stopped in front of me, as his fellow demon of the slums moved to my right to cut off the rest of the sidewalk.

"You slumming man?" asked the tall one.

"Friend, most of us are only a paycheque or two from the proverbial gutter. Problem is, hoods like you two are the poster boys for the media that paints all ghetto dwellers as social parasites. You give the ghetto a bad name."

The shorter one arched his eyebrows and said, "don't be cute. A man dressed like you don't got no business down here except to cause trouble."

Surprised that I wasn't intimidated, the tall one arched his back to stand straighter and bellowed, "man your lip can be buttoned if I don't like what I hear."

I leaned toward him, almost close enough for him to feel my breath. "Son, you try to button my lip, and you will spend the rest of the night trying to pick up your teeth off the sidewalk. I'm not a man you want to mess with, believe me."

They reached into their pant's pockets and came out with switch blades. I smiled and brought out the big bastard of a 45 and levelled it at them while saying, "now boys, if you want to play games, my friend and I know how to play.

If you want to go home and let mommy change your diapers, me and my friend are willing to let it pass this time."

They stood there with their mouths hanging open like they had just seen a ghost. Hell, maybe that's what I was, a ghost sent up from hell to stomp all over the bastards who tried to rule the world with force and power. I could stop them, because I could be just as cruel and merciless as they were.

They separated and made a path for me between them. As I passed them with the 45 still in my hand, I said, "goodnight boys."

I walked through the rotting and marred doors into what was, no doubt, once a grand and glorious hotel. Like the human beings of America, who served their corporate masters, the once architecturally splendorous edifice had served its purpose, so it had been discarded and allowed to deteriorate. It was just another monument to a society that itself was in decay and decline.

I walked across the stained marble floor to the reception desk, where a clerk who looked like a steel rail that had lost its resiliency, glared at me with eyes so deep set you needed a magnifying glass to see how far they went back into his head. He was probably forty-five, but looked seventy-five. One look at his needle scarred arms told the story. He was only a living, breathing shell of what used to be a man. The needle had taken away his senses, and now he was only another fish in the endless sea of misery and despair. He had a bottle of shoe polish in front of him with the cap off and a black stain from the polish glistened slightly on his lips. He was about as low as a man could get, but a society that lived off human misery would try its damnest to get him lower. If he was lucky, he would die tomorrow or maybe the next day, but the chances were he'd trudge on a few more years, until his body was finally eaten up and could resist death no longer.

Grinning through dark, rotted teeth, he smilingly said, "coming for a blow job my man? All you up town guys like to get it done cheap don't you?"

Placing my right hand on the desk I was rather curt and abrupt with my reply. "Not tonight."

Surprised, he retorted. "OK, so you want to spend a little more."

He picked up the bottle of shoe polish, took a short swig and said, "I can get you a good lay then. There's a gal upstairs just lost her supply, and she'll go for a bottle of polish. Give me a buck, and I'll set it up for you."

A little perturbed, I leaned in a closer to him. "I'm here to see a friend."

"Oh, you must be here to see Jack. Damn, he must be good. All you fellows keep coming back to see him. Really does a good job, uh?"

"I want to see Paul Cross."

Reaching for the polish bottle again, he got a quizzical look on his face. "Paul Cross, man he ain't no good. I let him have me a few nights ago, and he's a real amateur when he drops to his knees. Don't have nowhere near the technique Jack does."

I bent over the counter and grabbed him by the collar of his dingy shirt and pulled him up close to me. The putrid smell of his breath nearly made me faint with disgust. I felt bad about accosting a poor slob who had been sacrificed at the altar of despair, but still said, "man, I am not here for sex. I want to see Paul Cross, and if you don't tell me what room he is in, I'm going to shove that bottle down your throat."

Shaking his head from side to side, he seemed to maintain his calm, and said, "O.K., O.K. man, he is in three-forty. But there ain't nobody up there but the broad, and she ain't much of a lay. Hell, most guys wind up in bed with Paul rather than go to bed with the old hag."

Fall From Apocalypse

I let him loose. Just as I took my hands off his collar he spat in my face and said, "goddamn motherfucker, I'm gonna kill your ass," as he reached under the counter and came out with a gun.

I reached up with my left hand and swatted the gun in his right hand away with a wide sweeping motion. The gun hit the floor behind the counter but did not go-off. He was still spitting at me when I reached down, picked up the bottle of polish and poured it over his head, then pushed him back hard against the wall. I looked down at the gun on the floor, then nonchalantly up at him as he was now shivering with fright and said, "you pick that up and I am going to rip your balls off and shove 'um down your throat."

He stared at me with daggers in his eyes, but never moved. I turned, walked to the stairs and headed up to the third floor. The carpet on the stairs was ripped and torn. The walls were crusted with dark brown debris and each step seemed to be taking me somewhere I didn't really want to go.

I knocked on Paul's door but got no answer. The door was slightly ajar, so I gave it a nudge and walked inside. A woman in her birthday suit was sitting on the sofa sipping on a cheap bottle of wine. She looked like one of the witches from the opening scene of Macbeth.

"Paul ain't here, and I ain't in the mood. Blow man."

I replied in a serious tone. "I'm a friend of Paul's from the war. I'd like to see him."

Weaving her upper torso back and forth, as she gently fondled a sagging, but still voluptuous right breast, she said, "the war? God, which one? You mean the bang-bang war or the war for juice?"

"Is Paul on the stuff?"

Still fondling her breast, she seemed to be enjoying herself. "On the stuff? He ain't never been off it."

"Where is he now?"

Almost laughing out loud, she continued to weave back and forth while still playing with her breast. "Hell, he had a date with some fellow in fancy clothes like you. Gave Paul a ten-spot to go to the movies and home for some extra-curricular activities afterward. The kind of guy Paul really goes for. Hell, he might fall in love with the guy. Paul is real emotional about these things. He falls for too many of 'um. He got hung up on a guy a couples of months ago and left for three weeks. Left me here all alone to take care of myself. You want to lay me? Hell, I ain't got nothing else to do. You name the price – fifty cents, a dollar. Whatever you want to give me."

Getting perturbed, I was rather direct. "I'm not here to lay anybody my friend. All I want to do is see Paul and find out what the hell is going on?"

I must admit that I was enjoying watching her massage her breast. I coughed and said, "I see Paul in downtown Manhattan, and he is wearing an expensive suit. He tells me he is rolling in dough. Then, I find out he is living in a dump like this."

She stopped weaving, leaned back and let out a roaring laugh. She grabbed a wine bottle setting on the table beside her, provocatively spread her legs, exposing a well manicured snatch and wedged the bottle between her thighs.

"Paul in an expensive suit. That's a real laugh mister, a real laugh. You a comedian or something?"

She spread her legs a little wider and began to work the butt of the bottle between her ever-widening legs. Damn, she had really been through the mill. There was enough room up there for two wine bottles and a magnum of champagne.

Fall From Apocalypse

She slowly raised her chin toward the ceiling, sighed erotically and said, "man, I am kinda hot for you. Suppose I give it to you for free. How about it?"

Smiling, I replied, "looks like you are doing a pretty good job yourself."

Lowering her head and looking directly at me with what were still beautiful brown eyes, she said, "yeah, I get my kicks doing it this way sometimes, because I rarely get anything this big in my cute huge love nest."

Continuing to push and frantically twist the bottle into herself, she began to buck up to meet each thrust. She sighed long and deep again, her eyes rolled back into her head and she said, "most men just don't measure up to take care of a huge tunnel of love like I have. Maybe you can. I am tired of Paul always getting the big ones. He is a cock hog. Come on man, let me see what you got. Unzip those pants and give it to me good."

I asked, "how long you and Paul been married?"

"Married, hell man. I'm his sister."

Goddamn, what kind of bastard was Paul? I thought I knew him, but this was not the Paul

Fall From Apocalypse

Cross I knew. It had to be a mistake. This was the wrong Paul Cross."

"You got a picture of Paul?"

"Yeah, in the bedroom."

It was Paul Cross, alright. But this wasn't the Paul Cross I knew, living in incest with his sister.

I walked back into the living room, where the broad was in a real frenzy, twisting and jerking as she shoved more and more of the bottle up into herself.

I looked down at her and said, "baby, when you finish with your kicks, put some clothes on. I'll be back in a few minutes."

She looked up at me with a puzzled look. "Put something on? Hell man, I've got all I need on. What I need is something else warm and stiff in me. You some kind of nut? You a fetish freak? I ain't your girl if that's what you want. I'd just soon twist the bottle a few more times than let you tie me up or beat me."

"Listen, I don't have a fetish, and I don't want to lay you. All I want is to get you out of this place, buy you some decent clothes and put you up for the night at my place."

Fall From Apocalypse

"Where you live, doll?"

"Downtown Manhattan, Malbury off 63rd."

"Hey, you're a real big shot."

I smiled at the thought of being a big shot. Hey, compared to the dump she was living in, maybe she was right. Maybe, to her, I was a big shot.

I said rather nonchalantly, "get dressed. I'll go down to the desk and call a cab."

She sat and stared in disbelief as I walked out the door. She must have been beautiful once. Maybe she still was if she could be given a chance to get out of the squalor and misery.

As I was heading toward the stairs, I saw the two hoods I'd met earlier come out of a room at the end of the hall right by the stairs. They had that glazed look that meant they had just shot up.

The clerk was not there, so I just used the phone and called a cab. On the way back up, I passed the room the two hoods came out of, and since the door was ajar, I peaked in. Two women were sitting on the sofa wrapped in each others arms passionately kissing. In a nearby chair, a man was sticking a needle into his left arm. Hell, I thought, why should I judge him? The rich were doing the same thing. The only difference was that they got doctors to write them prescriptions for corporate-manufactured drugs. Down in the ghetto, they enriched their local drug dealer, rather than the big-moneyed boys in the board rooms.

I walked down the hallway to Paul's room, and his sister was there waiting for me in a tight fitting nylon dress that hugged her ample but sexy hips like it had been painted on her torso. She smiled and said, "hey, I thought maybe you had changed your mind. I even got in the shower to sober up a little. First time I've been this sober in a long time."

I smiled back, but just as I was about to say something the door sprang wide open and the two hoods were on me before I had a chance to pull my big bastard of a forty-five. One of the bastards held me at bay with a switch blade while the other removed my gun from the shoulder holster.

Handing the gun to his buddy, who was grinning broadly through rotten teeth, the bastard said, "keep him covered Joe, while me and the broad has a little fun."

With a measured, assured tone, I whispered softly, "you touch her asshole, and you will have to answer to me, and that will not be a pleasant experience."

The bastard licked his lips and replied, "you ain't gonna do nothing. My friend there with your gun will blow your balls off if you mess with us."

The girl, almost pleading, said, "let him go. I'll do anything you want."

Sticking his chest out and taking a cocky stance in front of her, the bastard was really sure of himself. "Now, you just do what I say baby, and maybe we will let him outta here in one piece. Speaking of piece, take them goddamn clothes off. Let's see some tit and ass. I am ready for some action."

Paul's sister slipped out of her dress, and the fact that she had no bra or panties on really excited the bastard, because he immediately unzipped his pants and his love-stick was already at full-mast. She dropped to her knees and took the root of his passion in her mouth. She was trying to give me a chance to get out of the situation the best way she knew how. What the hell I thought. She had probably done a lot worse. But by-God, she had never been forced to submit in front of Aaron Adams. The bastards, the goddamn bastards.

The asshole squeezed and manipulated her breasts while the other son-of-bitch backed up to get a better view of the action. Too bad he didn't do his job. He took his eyes off me for a split second and I had him. I let out a deafening scream and grabbed his gun hand, tilting the barrel down toward the floor. I stepped hard on his foot, and he collapsed in pain.

While I snapped the bastard's wrist and took the gun from him, Paul's sister bit hell out of the other guys manhood. By the time they both regained their composure, the girl was standing beside me and the two bastards were looking down the barrel of my forty-five.

With my left hand, I motioned for her to go into the hallway. She was a good kid. She never said a word, just picked up her dress, put it on and went into the hallway.

Smiling sinisterly, I said, "OK boys, I'm going to play a little game. You really like sex, uh? Drop your pants, and wobble over to the window."

I reached down and raised the window with my left hand and took a deep breath of fresh air. Again, letting that sinister smile slowly creep across my lips, I could see they were really scared.

"Fine boys, fine. Lay those beauts on the window sill. Damn, you got a couple of nice ones. I bet you're real proud of them. You should be. Yes sir, you should be."

Fall From Apocalypse

They were shaking like a sinner who had just received the holy spirit at an old-fashioned revival meeting. Still smiling broadly, I said, "boys, I could get really tough, but I know you're genuinely sorry for what you did to the young lady, so I'm going to make you stand here in front of the window with your pants down and those magnificent, huge specimens of manhood sticking out the window for an hour as punishment for your nasty little deed. Of course, its awfully damn cold isn't it? I can just feel the chill in the air. I wouldn't want you boys to catch a cold."

Then I slowly obliterated the smile from my face and gave them the death stare with piercing, penetrating eyes that seemed to flicker with evil intent. I put my hand on the window, and suddenly, without warning, I pulled it down, and it fell on their manhood like a guillotine slicing Marie Antoinette's neck. They stood there screaming in pain but couldn't move for fear of hurting themselves more.

"Goodnight boys."

J. Wayne Frye

CHAPTER 3
THE FUN HAD JUST STARTED

B.J. was waiting for me, and I decided it might be better if Alicia Cross stayed with her. As B.J. left with her, she stopped at the door and flashed that *I'm hot for you* look my way.

I flopped back in my desk chair, propped up my feet and went back over the day's events. Paul Cross, an old army buddy who looked like he was rolling in dough the last time I saw him was living in an incestuous relationship with his sister in a dump off the Bowery. To top it off, he was gay. I had always believed everybody should do their own thing, but I had shared a foxhole and a bunk with the guy for 13 months in Nam, and there was no indication whatsoever. Alicia Cross would have to provide some answers in the morning. I lowered my head and dozed off into a deep slumber.

The sound of the phone ringing made me nearly tumble out of my chair. I managed to keep from falling and grabbed the phone. "Adam's Investigations."

The voice on the other end was my friend from the 87th Precinct, John Havoc. He was a tough cop, but a damn good man who, unlike too many cops, cared about people. He bellowed, "why the hell aren't you home at 5:00 AM?"

"Well hell, Jack. This place is more home than home."

His voice became a little more tense. "Ever heard of Fluke Williams?"

"Yeah, syndicate torpedo, I believe."

"Believe hell. You know goddamn well who he is. And furthermore Aaron, you are the prime suspect in his death."

"Wait a damn minute. I'm a private citizen and a taxpayer. I don't like no cop calling me up at 5:00 AM to accuse me of murder just because I have put a few guys on the slab in the past. Guys who deserved it I might add."

"Get the hell off your high-horse, Aaron. You left your calling card."

Really getting irritated, I replied, "you want to get to the point or do you just want to tie my line up all morning?"

Sounding really serious now, John cut lose with a tirade of vindictiveness. "Fluke Williams was one of the syndicates top killers for hire. We figure he was brought in from L.A. for one quick job, but the guy he was after was a little too smart. Now, we know you have been hired by the Merchants' Association to find Bob Clacy's killer.

Fall From Apocalypse

Seems like this made you a target for the syndicate, since you were putting a stop to their extortion and protection racket. Then there is the way Williams got it, definitely Adam's style. He was drilled a couple of times – real neatly, so he would be conscious for the grand finale. We picked up what was left of him in a trash can off 43rd Street. It took a pretty sadistic bastard to kill like that."

"Your goddamn right, but I'm not the only sadistic bastard in town. Hell, you and I know he got exactly what he deserved. The organization is the real sadist, along with the bankers and stock manipulators on Wall Street. Somebody should start taking care of the real crooks on Wall Street. One thing for sure, the cops and the government ain't going to do nothing to them, and they do very damn little to fight organized crime. Just enough to make the public think they are looking after the people's interests. Well, I've got the bankers, the stock brokers, the financiers and the syndicates numbers, and I am not afraid of any of them. Any of mess with me and they got real trouble."

I paused a bit to catch my breath and continued. "Mind you, I am not admitting to any kill. If you can pin it on me – go ahead, but when they send a torpedo after me, they better come spitting lead from both hands, because I don't go easy. Now, you can tell those ass-kissing politicians you work for that Aaron Adams said they could all shove it."

Dead serious, John replied, "we're going to pin one on you someday, Aaron. Mark my words, your day is coming. You've got off one time too many."

"John, you're a fine cop, but you're only one guy. You are stuck in the middle between boys in the department kissing ass to get ahead and the screwed up politicians taking the city and the people for every goddamn thing they can. Meanwhile, most of the cops are no better than the people they are arresting. Half of you are on the take in one form or another, and you are out keeping the rest of us in line. Boy, don't play your tough-guy routine with me. I'm tougher than all of you."

John simply said "good bye" and hung up.

I took a quick shower and shave in the office bathroom and slipped into the spare suit I kept at the office for emergencies. I caught the uptown express and got off a couple of blocks below B.J.'s apartment, so the morning air could slap me in the face for a few minutes. As I walked the few blocks to B.J.'s apartment, I noticed clouds forming overhead, obliterating the morning sun that often beat down so heavily on the pavement that you could see heat rising precipitously from the asphalt.

Fall From Apocalypse

B.J. lived in a nice neighbourhood. Take a 15 minute subway ride, and you were out of the jungles of concrete and steel. The Bowery was far behind. The frictions of racial strife became a distant concern. The ghettos of despair faded into the deep recesses of the mind. Yet, you could sense that the tide was changing. The tentacles of the city were reaching out in every direction to bring more and more people into the muck and slime of corruptive strife and turmoil. The 1960's were just another decade of U.S. government manipulative fear-mongering to keep the populace under control. The gullible public fell for the propaganda, believing that there was always some evil empire out to destroy America. They were too stupid to realize the problem in the world was the USA, not the Soviet Union, not Cuba, not North Korea, not Vietnam. The Americans were the most easily manipulated people in the world. How many fathers and mothers encouraged their children to sign-up to fight the evil commies in Vietnam, when what the people really needed to fight was their own repressive government. Freedom – most Americans had no idea what it really was. They had been brainwashed into believing they were the freest people in the world, but they could not see the invisible chains and shackles they willingly lined up to have placed on them. There was no hope for a people who snapped to attention and dutifully placed their hands over their hearts to pledge allegiance to an idea that didn't really exist.

Fall From Apocalypse

1969 was a year of turmoil. Americans had once again put a man into the White House who only answered to the barons of greed. Richard Nixon was as devious as any man who ever held the office of President, and I knew that freedom would suffer mightily over the coming years, and that red-baiting would be used as a tool of fear to keep the public from demanding justice where there was none. Oh, how I longed to escape the coming calamities that would imprison the populace to the corporations that were beginning their inexorable march to complete control of a government that only bowed before those with wealth and power, while ignoring the real needs of the real people.

Then my mind began to wander over the events of the past few days. Paul Cross and I were friends, or, at least had been friends in a the army. Strangely, I believed in conscription, because as long as you had people in the military who did not want to be there, there was a built-in safety valve. Paul and I hated the army, and all it stood for in a world that had to bow before the mightiest military machine ever known to man. The only way left for other countries or individuals with just causes to stand against the U.S. military machine was through terrorist acts. Yet, which was a greater act of terrorism, the lone guy who straps explosives to his body, or a country that drops bombs from 80,000 feet to force others into submission?

Fall From Apocalypse

Paul Cross was now an anomaly to me, and his sister was going to provide some answers. I was going to find out the truth about him.

B..J lived in an old brownstone that had been converted into apartments, when the owners wealth finally ran out. Mrs. Kirsh was a grand old lady, but a bit eccentric. She was already out working in her patch of flowers when I strolled up the walkway.

"Mr. Adams, I do declare. How nice to see you," she said as she looked up with a spade in her hand.

"Good morning, Mrs. Kirsh."

Smiling and pointing the spade at me, she said, "why how strange to see you going up to Miss Holden's apartment at this time of the morning. Seems to me that a young, virile looking man like you should be coming down instead of going up."

"I am not that young, nor am I as virile as I used to be."

Mrs. Kirsh got a contemplative look on her face. "I thought you were up there last night."

"No, it was just a friend of hers who spent the night."

"Hmm, maybe you've been slipping up a bit."

Fall From Apocalypse

"It was a woman with her, Mrs. Kirsh."

"Well, I am not one to pry, but I do like you, so I suggest you treat Miss Holden right, young man. There were two gents went up there about midnight. I never heard them come down, and there were some real wild sounds up there. Having a real party, I would say. I figured it was you and a friend, maybe. Definitely two males though, cause I was coming out my door about the time they got to the top of the stairs. I'd swear one of those fellows looked like you from the back."

Somewhat concerned, I replied, "maybe I better check things out. I'll keep you posted Mrs. Kirsh."

"Don't get too angry, now. All we gals like to spread our wings now and then."

As I climbed the stairs to B.J.'s apartment, it hit me like a winter morning when you walk out of a warm house into the bitter cold. I was afraid, afraid that she might be playing around. Son-of-bitch, it hit me. I loved the woman. Aaron Adams, the don't-give-a-damn tough guy was in love. Damn, I was going soft. I had finally found something worthwhile. I had found something worth coming home to, something to love and caress after mingling in the gutters with the scum who corrupted and destroyed. Yeah, I was going soft alright, but it was the kind of soft I wanted. The kind of soft I needed.

Fall From Apocalypse

She would be lying there, waiting for me to taste the delights that so many others had tasted before me, but would never taste again. Or would she? Just what the hell were two men doing up there after midnight?

The half-opened door gave me my answer. My heart plummeted towards my feet. The blood rushed to my head, and I caught the vomit half up the esophagus. She was on the floor, Alecia Cross's nude body was hacked up like some weird caricature in a circus of horrors. I nearly fell several times in my mad flight to B.J.'s bedroom.

She was tied spread-eagled on the bed, her feet and legs tied down, and her nude body was bruised around the thighs and breasts, but she was breathing. She was breathing!

I quickly untied her, removed the gag from her mouth, ran to the door and called Mrs. Kirsh. On the way back, I grabbed the slip cover off the sofa, tossed it over Alecia's body and called an ambulance.

Mrs. Kirsh became hysterical, but I finally calmed her down enough to help me dress B.J. I was worried. B.J. had not said a word, not even moaned. Fortunately, we were in a nice neighbourhood, so the ambulance was there in 10 minutes. Had we been in the ghetto, no doubt, we would have had to wait much longer.

Fall From Apocalypse

While B.J. was still in emergency, John Havoc burst into the waiting room and demanded in a loud voice, "where is she?"

Mrs. Kirsh started to reply, but before she could get it out, John turned to me. "You son-of-a-bitch, you are the cause of this. I know you are. You have pissed off the wrong people with your arrogance, and they have gone after her."

Not one to take tirades well, I replied, "shut up. I don't need this vindictive display of emotion right now."

"Listen. Don't get tough with me. If she doesn't make it, I'll take care of you personally."

Mrs. Kirsh, trying to be the peace maker, said, "boys, boys, please."

Calming down a bit, I turned to Mrs. Kirsh. "Sorry, Mrs. Kirsh. You see, John here is in love with B.J. Problem is, he can't figure out why she prefers me to him."

John stared at me with an intense rage, as the doctor walked into the room. "Mr. Adams?"

"Yeah, yeah, " I replied.

"She will be alright, just a slight concussion, some bruising and contusions."

I breathed a sigh of relief, as he continued. "She was severely beaten, and well – well, whoever beat her used a blunt instrument to shove into her vagina, but that will heal in time, too. It was an incredibly vicious attack. She is lucky to be alive. She is asking for you, Mr. Adams. You may see her, but only a few minutes, though."

John was still seething with hate, as I looked back at him and let out with a big grin just to let him know I was the one she wanted to see, not him.

A big smile crept across her lips as I bent over to kiss her cheek.

"Hi tiger."

"B.J."

"Shhh… I know tiger. I know."

"Doc says you will be OK."

"They killed her didn't they, Aaron?"

"Yeah, pretty nasty job, I'm afraid."

"I knew it. They weren't interested in me. Tiger, please – don't go on a rampage."

"Don't worry, I'll let John handle it."

She gave me a concerned look. "Yeah, sure you will. Just be careful. These guys are dangerous. One of them must have been a pool shark. He kept shouting cue the bitch up, put it in her side pocket, and when he shoved that figurine up me, he kept laughing and shouting something about the bitch is a cue ball waiting to make a break."

"You get some sleep, baby. I'll start doing some laughing."

"Don't Aaron, please."

"I'll be alright baby. Just going to poke around a little."

I kissed her lightly, walked to the door and turned to smile at her again. She said, "hell, you are going to do what you're going to do. I might as well make it easier for you. Try Sharkey's Place."

"Sharkey's?"

"Yeah, one of them was smoking a Havana, a Monte Cristo. I only know one place where those are smuggled in – Sharkey's. Some government, uh. They think keeping Americans from smoking Cuban cigars will bring Castro to his knees."

"You should be a private dick, baby."

"No, you be the dick."

Fall From Apocalypse

Smiling at her innuendo, I gently eased the door shut and headed back down the hall. I said goodbye to Mrs. Kirsh, who said she would stick around awhile.

I thanked her and started toward the exit, when John stepped out of an archway and grabbed me by the coat sleeve, motioning toward an anti-room. "In here guy, we got some talking to do."

"Make it quick. I'm in a hurry."

"Yeah, so were the boys at B.J.'s last night. It seems you forget there was another woman up there. Any idea who she was?"

"Alecia Cross. B.J. took her home as a favour. 1435 Lorton Street, in the Bowery. She lived there with her brother, Paul Cross. Friend of Paul's named Bill Lawrence gave me a retainer to go down and talk to Paul. That's it. The rest you know."

"Where's this Paul Cross, now?"

"Your guess is as good as mine. You're a damn cop. Find him."

"OK, big boy. You might be clean on this one, but don't try to go after these guys on your own. I'll have your ticket and maybe your hide to go with it. You got me?

"Don't play the tough cop routine with me. I'm tougher and meaner and don't give a damn. You know it, I know it, and the guys who did this are gonna know it. I'm busy. If you want to contact me, you've got my phone number."

"I'm warning you, Aaron."

His voice trailed off as I turned and walked out the door toward vengeance.

Sharkey ran a pretty clean place, but, like all small businessmen in a country that was only concerned with helping the corporations, he had to dabble in a few nefarious things to keep his head above water. One of those things was smuggling in Cuban cigars for those who didn't care if a quality product was made by a communist or an American corporate wage slave. That is the American government for you. Hell, they had tried to embargo the Cuban government out of existence for years, but Castro and his people were just too tough for them. One day, maybe the U.S. government would come to its senses, and stop trying to shove corporate culture down the Cubans' throats. Oh yeah, it was supposed to be about democracy. What a lie. Hell, America could use a little bit of democracy itself before trying to export it all over the world. What the government was really exporting was corporate domination of the entire world – American style. The culture of greed was what it was really all about.

Fall From Apocalypse

I often wondered just how important democracy was to the ghetto kid with an empty belly in a country that didn't give a damn about the poor. How appropriate that the government went after the small-time criminals, but let the corporate criminals rob and plunder with complete impunity. And the syndicate was a big corporation – a criminal enterprise that was a target of the government only when it wanted to divert the population's attention from the real criminals in the boardrooms of America. Well, Aaron Adams wasn't afraid of either of them. I was one man who would fight them on their own terms, on their own ground, in any way possible. I would go toe-to-toe, eye-to-eye, in a head-on battle of mutual cruelty and hatred.

Sharkey beamed a smile my way, "hey, hey, Aaron Adams."

"Hello, Sharkey."

"Hey, where's that secretary of yours? That is one dame I like to see in my place. She is one classy woman, and I'll bet one helluva secretary, uh?"

"Right on all accounts Sharkey, but she is in Queens Receiving right now."

With a look of concern, Sharkey said, "nothing serious, I hope."

"She'll be OK. Couple of hoods took another woman out who was with her, though."

"Goddamn! You gonna take 'um, uh Adams?"

"Going to give it my best shot."

"Goddamn right, man. Let the sons-a-bitches have it good and proper, Aaron Adams style. Goddamn cops won't do nothing unless its some rich person."

I leaned on Sharkey's counter. "Sell many Monte Cristos?"

"Hell, yeah. The stupid US government is busy embargoing Cuba, which just makes the public want them cigars even more. Embargo is good for my business."

"One of the hoods was smoking a Monte Cristo, and this would be the only place he could have gotten it."

Beaming now, Sharkey said, "hey, I got it. Sure, I'd like to help, but I sell at least 100 a day. Hell, one guy buys 50 a week."

"This guy is probably a pool shark, and likes to talk hip pool language."

"Pool shark, uh?"

"Any description?"

"Hell no. I was so upset about the beating she took that I didn't even ask. Some detective, uh?"

Sharkey, with a quizzical look on his face, said, "think he might have bought it last night?"

"Maybe, they went up to B.J.'s after midnight."

"Sold only one after six yesterday. A real pool hound he is, too. Little crazy, if you ask me. He works for Cassidy. Could be your boy. Harold Lasky."

"Address?"

No, but he usually comes in here on Thursdays. Today? Probably over at Manny's. Big game there on Fridays. Starts early afternoon. You know the place?"

"Yeah, and thanks Sharkey."

"Sure, tell B.J. I'll be looking for her real soon. This place could use a little of her type class."

Manny's was a few blocks down from Sharkey's, but it was a different world. Down Murrell to 21st, then 22nd , and you went from grey to black. Sharkey's was an uptown joint compared to Manny's.

Fall From Apocalypse

A pot-head, who was weaving and bobbing his head, leaned over a cash register that was set up on a piece of dry wall propped up on cinder blocks, greeted me nonchalantly with a wave of the hand as I walked into Manny's. "Sorry man, all the tables is took. Fridays is our big day. Try back a little later."

I was probably a little curt. "No game man. I'm looking for Harold Lasky."

He smiled through what was left of his teeth, making me think how simple things like a visit to the dentist were beyond the meagre financial means of most Americans. A stream of saliva ran down his chin, as he said, "I ain't never heard of the dude."

Now, I was getting a little perturbed. "You heard of him. Is he here?"

His head still weaving back and forth, almost like he was in a trance, the clerk murmured, "listen fella, you better watch your manners. No gook in a suit comes in here and talks to me like that."

Now, I was beginning to get really annoyed. I leaned over the drywall make-shift desk, grabbed him by his shirt collar, pulled him off his feet and peered straight into his eyes, "Lasky, Harold Lasky. Is he here?"

Fall From Apocalypse

Suddenly seeming more coherent, he replied, "yeah, yeah, back room through the blue door over there," as he pointed frantically, his finger shaking violently.

Letting go of him, I said, "thank you."

I eased the door open, sled in unnoticed, then slammed the hell out of the door to get their attention. The four goons in the room all cocked their heads my way.

"Hi boys. Need to talk to Harold Lasky."

One really cocky looking fellow with a face full of pock-marks bellowed, "what the hell for, asshole?"

Very calmly, I said, "you Lasky?"

"Maybe, maybe not. You heard me. How come you wanna talk to him?"

"Buddy, I am in no mood to be messed with. I simply want to have a few words with him. That's it."

One of the goons began to stealthily move across the room toward me. Like I wouldn't notice him. What an idiot. Meanwhile, the other three let smiles creep across their faces in anticipation of the coming rumble.

The pock-faced one said, "you better turn around and get outta here."

I gave them a big grin, reached under my coat and brought out the cannon. They all froze with fear, too scared to move as I said, "one more time, Lasky, Harold Lasky."

The one who had been edging my way wheeled around and pointed his finger at a tall, skinny guy with a pool cue in his hand. "Him. Him. Goddamn man, that's him."

Lasky's chest began to rise as he took on a tough demeanour to impress his comrades. "Hell yes, I'm Lasky. These shit-heads ain't got no guts. I ain't afraid of you or your gun. I ain't done nothing copper. I'm clean. I tell you, I'm clean."

Very calmly, I replied, "sure Lasky, but we'll talk about it, uh?"

"Talk's cheap man. Sure."

I eased the forty-five back in the shoulder holster and walked over to Lasky. Pointing at the back door, I said, "that door lead into the alley?"

"Yeah, sure."

Again pointing at the door, I said, "let's talk in private."

Fall From Apocalypse

"Sure man, Sure." Then looking at the others, he continued, "you fellas go ahead and play. Me and the dude is gonna talk."

We moved into the alley, and I gently closed the door behind us, noticing that there was no knob on the outside. I was very direct. "Holden. B.J. Holden."

He got a look of intense fear on his face and uttered, "never, never."

I crushed the cigar that was dangling out of his mouth into his face with the palm of my right hand and gave him a slap or two across the puss.

Now, he was really frightened as he screamed, "you ain't no cop."

"Alecia Cross," I said as I gave him another backhand.

"I never. I never," he pleaded.

"Paul Cross. You ever heard of him?"

"No. No."

"You goddamn son-of-a-bitch. Talk or I will mop this alley up with your hide."

"Who, who the hell are you, man?

"I am Aaron Adams, asshole."

He looked like he was having a heart attack as he uttered, "Adams, Aaron Adams. Oh, God! Listen to me. Please listen. I never touched either one of 'um. You hear me – never touched 'um. I swear. I swear."

I backed off just a little bit, stared straight into his eyes and said, "you son-of-a-bitch. Who the hell are you kidding?"

He started to move toward me, but I stomped hell out of his foot, pushed him back against the wall and leaned in real close, as I almost whispered, "who was with you?"

Nervously shaking, he muttered, "Tornlison. Mark Tornlison. John Cassidy sent us. Told us Cross's sister had to be took out."

Then, in so close I could smell his putrid breath, I continued, "why?"

"Man, we don't ask John no questions. Just do the job. That's all. But you gotta believe me. I never touched 'um."

At that moment I knew the son-of-a-bitch was going to die. No ifs, ands or buts. He had put his lousy hands on B.J., and nobody did that and got away with it, as long as I had breath.

Fall From Apocalypse

I backed off just a bit, but he knew what was coming. Then, he said, "OK, asshole. I did it, and I enjoyed it. I love fucking-up a woman real good. It is my favourite thing in the whole world. I…."

I didn't give him a chance to finish. I kicked his feet from under him, and he dropped to the ground. He tried to get up, but it was a waste of time. He only wound up back down again.

I stuck my left foot in his rib cage and bore down with all my weight. His chest collapsed and blood spurted out his mouth, as he gasped for a breath that never came. I grabbed him by the feet, swung him over my left shoulder and battered his head against the wall until there was nothing left to batter.

I stepped over his mangled body and headed out of the alley. The organization would think twice before it messed with B.J. again. Aaron Adams had just left a message of blood, and if any more of them tried to hurt B.J., the city's street sweepers would be out of a job, because I would mop the whole city up with the sons-a-bitches. Next was Tornlison. Then, there was Cassidy. Hell, the fun had just started.

CHAPTER 4
THE BOX

"Feeling better, baby?" I said as B.J. smiled up at me.

"Sure, now that you are here. What time is it?"

"Little passed 11:00. You got somewhere you need to be?"

"Just want to be in your arms. That's all."

Smiling at the thought of feeling her warm body next to me, I said, "you look like a million dollars, baby."

Winking at me with her left eye, she said, "old bills, maybe."

"Crisp, new ones"

"They say I can go home in a few days," she said as she looked down between her legs and continued, "you will have to go a little easy down there for awhile."

"What did those bastards use on you?

"Chinese figurine from my night stand."

"The bastards."

Fall From Apocalypse

"Oh, I don't know. It kind of tickled at first."

"Don't joke about it."

"Sorry, Tiger. You found them yet?"

"One of them."

"Talk?"

"A little."

"Going to ever talk again?"

"In hell."

"You promised."

"You know my promises aren't worth a damn."

She looked directly into my eyes. Damn near burned a hole in them with her stare. "I love you, tiger."

I let a slow grin creep across my face. "You better."

"Why?"

"I can't afford a new secretary."

"Bastard."

Fall From Apocalypse

I took her hand in mine. "Feel like going over it?"

"There's not much to go over. We had settled down for the night. We were both not bashful. Like me, she sleeps naked. We were sitting in front of the TV, catching the news. We were talking when I looked up at the door and realized that I had left the night latch off and the door unlocked. As I started to get up, the door sprang open and in walked two torpedoes with cannons levelled at us."

She eased up in the bed and continued. "Learned my lesson about going nude. That must have really been what set them off. One of them damn near broke his finger trying to unzip his pants. Don't know what really happened to Alecia. The fast guy had her on the floor humping away. She fought a little, but he slapped her damn near unconscious. I figured I could lure the other one into the bedroom with a bitch-in-heat routine and possibly get my gun. I laid on the come-hither look, and he went ape-shit with desire. Anyway, I told him I really needed to get laid bad. He dropped his pants, shirt, gun – the works and followed me into the bedroom. I got him into a passionate embrace, started to kiss him and jammed my knee into his groin. By the time I got to the drawer for my gun, the other bastard came in and kicked me in the ass so hard I nearly went through the wall."

Fall From Apocalypse

By then, I was seething with anger, but B.J. continued. "He stood over me, pulled the drawer open, looked down at my gun and laughed. The other one crawled up off the floor and slapped me a few times. Then they tossed me on the bed and really started working me over. They both raped me a couple of times until they were spent. Then they started with the figurine. I guess they figured I was finished. I passed out before I could reach the phone. Alecia was a good kid Aaron."

"Yes, and there are a lot of people going to pay for what they did to her and you."

"How to you figure it?"

'The torpedoes were back-street hoods, nothing big time, but the organization – the syndicate was the mover. Jack Cassidy, the hood who runs the Silver Dollar off 42nd and the Americas, made the contract."

"But why?"

"Damned if I know. Paul Cross should have the answer, but where the hell is he?"

Quizzically, B.J. said, "you could go back to the hotel on Lorton."

"No need, he'll read about the rub-out in the papers. He won't go back there. Chances are that he'll blow town, but he will give me a call. Yeah, he should give me a call."

"Why would he call you? He wasn't even the one who asked for help."

"Yeah, you may be right. Maybe Bill Lawrence is the guy who will call me."

Smiling, B.J. said, "you don't have to wait for him to call you. His number is on the phone message pad. Check my desk."

I got up, bent over and gave her a kiss. "See you later, baby."

"Keep growling, tiger."

My spirits were lifted. A few brief minutes with her and she put a new spark into my life. In fact, she was my life. Damn, and the organization nearly took her from me. They would pay. And the payment would be made in the only currency they understood, blood. Like the U.S. government, they engaged in nefarious acts to suck the life out of those who had no power to stand against tyranny. Well, I had no power, but I did have a firty-five that spit out retribution in lead.

As I strolled toward my office, the dark of the early morning city seemed to embrace me like a long lost friend. I was home in that dark. I liked it.

Fall From Apocalypse

The office was on the eighth floor of an old twenty story building in lower Manhattan. It was only seven o'clock, but as the darkness of the early morning began to slowly fade, a few of those who got to work early were already gathering at the snack bar for their morning dose of drugs. Yeah, many of these people who could not start the day without an oral injection of caffeine probably looked with disdain on the drug addicts who sought relief from a society that oppressed and overwhelmed them until their only escape was the euphoria offered by illicit drugs. Yet, those who bought corporate drugs were not drug addicts, just good consumers who oiled the machinery of capitalism.

I stopped by Larry's News-A-Rama and picked up a morning newspaper. On the way up in the elevator that was slower than molasses running up hill, I glanced at the headlines. *Russians Break off Talks with U.S., U.S. Planes Bomb Civilians by Mistake, U.S. Fears China Missiles Can Reach California, U.S. Says No to North Vietnam Plea for Peace Talks.* Hey, it was 1969. The entire planet was in turmoil as the good old USA and that monolith of evil, the Soviet Union, were engaged in a fierce battle to see who could control the world. Russian communism, which, in reality was not communism at all, as it was an abomination to everything suggested by Marx and Engels, was the evil empire, but the USA was the knight in shining armour that was trying to rescue the world from the evils of a system not based on the principles of greed. Hey, corporations always had the people's best interests in mind. Everyone knew that. Yeah, and they really took good care of their employees, too. Treated them like royalty.

Yet, the people in both countries were powerless to change things as long as they lined up to be manacled with invisible chains in service to their masters. Free!!! What a laugh. Americans actually thought they were free. Demonstrate against an illegal and immoral war, and while your head is being bashed in by the Gestapo cops of America, who represent the powerful and wealthy, ask yourself how free you are. Try to start a business, only to be forced out by a predatory corporation that makes it impossible for you to compete, and ask how free you are. Try to be an atheist in a country that has freedom of religion, but not freedom from religion, and ask yourself how free you are. Try to stand against the military-industrial complex and see how responsive the government is. Try to demand equality of opportunity for all Americans and while the politicians pay lip-service to the idea, watch how rules are promulgated to make certain that the poor receive no justice, while the rich and powerful are handed everything on a silver platter. Freedom!!! Americans had no concept of what it really was, but they swallowed the propaganda dispensed by the government and the corporate media like a newborn suckling on a breast.

Fall From Apocalypse

To the kid with a bloated belly in the Mississippi backwater, to the ghetto dwelling mother of a newborn she was forced to have because the Christians don't want abortion, to the factory worker who toils for sustenance while his bosses live the high life, to the poor conscripted soldier who fights in a far off land while the children of the politicians who sent him there enjoy deferments from service, the idea of freedom is illusionary, only they don't know it. Most of those who have no chance of crawling out of the deep hole of poverty the system places them in actually believed in the lie promulgated by politicians that opportunity is there for all who want to grab it. What a distortion! Yeah, it is there for 1 out of 10,000 who claw their way out of abject poverty, but success, as well as freedom, was primarily available for all who are born into wealth and power. Nepotism opened more doors than ability.

Then, there was organized crime, "the organization." They were at the core of all that was wrong according to the government, but the government did nothing about it, because the organization owned the politicians just like the corporations. Anyway, the organization was no different than the bankers, corporate CEO's and the wall street barons of greed who robbed people every day. The only difference was that they were actually branded criminals by the government while the bankers and wall street tycoons were merely captains of industry. Meanwhile, they all preyed on the average Joe who struggled to keep his head above water in a system where all the cards were stacked against him.

Well, these people might be pulling the strings of manipulation for others, but Aaron Adams was different. Nobody pulled my strings. I was one son-of-bitch who just didn't give a damn.

I stepped off the elevator, walked toward the office and as I started to throw the paper in the hallway trashcan, something in the lower right hand corner of the front page caught my eye, *Two Men Slain.*

At first, I figured what the hell, that was no news in New York City, where half the populace was packing weapons of one type or another in a country that made it as easy to buy a gun as to pick up a pack of chewing gum at the local 7-11. Of course, the trigger-happy cops, who always shot first and asked questions later when they were patrolling the ghetto, didn't help matters.

I eased the paper back up gradually and skimmed the column for names. The two names seemed to leap off the page and pulsate in my brain – Bill Lawrence and Paul Cross.

I had to call John. Goddamn, this whole business was breaking wide open. I eased my office door open and got a real surprise. I nearly fell over the debris on the floor. My desk was turned over and the rest of the office looked like the village of My Lai after the American soldiers had obliterated, in a kill frenzy, everything in sight. Somebody was looking for something, but what?

I turned the desk back over, set the phone on it, pulled up a chair and gave John a ring. I had just started to open the undisturbed box of cigars Lawrence had left when Sergeant Peters answered the phone.

"Homicide, Sergeant Peters."

"Havoc, please."

Seemingly perturbed, Peters replied, "he's busy right now. May I help you?"

"Adams, Peters," I said as I decided to open the cigar box again.

Then I decided again to forgo the pleasure of a soothing smoke, when Peters said, "yeah, yeah, just a minute Aaron. He's been wanting to talk to you."

There was some mumbling in the background, and then John came on with his usual good cheer, obviously putting our somewhat acrimonious encounter at the hospital behind him. "Hello big boy. Got anybody ready for the morgue lately?"

A bit curt, I replied, "cut it John. I know about Cross and Lawrence. Saw it in the newspaper this morning. That is the extent of my knowledge, unfortunately. However, I do need some info from you."

"Since when does the department give out privileged information to private citizens?"

"I'm a taxpayer. I pay your salary. How about a little respect?"

"Respect, you don't pay enough taxes to get that. It's the big boys on Wall Street who get the respect."

"Hell, I pay a higher percentage in taxes than they do. We middle class suckers pick up the tab for them, so they can enjoy their Mercedes automobiles and yachts on our dollar. They really deserve it though, because they work so hard."

"Maybe you think we should go out and arrest them for being rich."

"Wouldn't be a bad idea, because you and I both know they are the really big crooks in this country, but they have too much juice to ever worry about jail time. John, I don't need to discuss the state of the economic structure in this screwed up country. I am telling you that there is something really big going on. Really big!"

"Yeah, so goddamn big you're liable to get your ticket lifted if you keep nosing around."

"John, I can help you. B.J. might be in danger. I refuse to let anything happen to her."

John, somewhat quizzically replied, "so, you think these are contract killings?"

"It's got the organization's prints all over it. You know it and so do I."

"Maybe, maybe not. I'll admit that it looked like a professional hit, but there are no threads to connect it to anybody, yet. It was a real neat job. Used only two slugs. Both of 'um got it in the back of the head, execution style."

"That's it?"

"Yeah, there clothes were removed after the kill and ripped apart. They were left lying beside the bodies."

With a knowing manner, I replied, "they were looking for something, and they wanted it bad."

Now, Havoc knew that I was on to something. "Bright boy, Aaron. By the way, we got another fresh corpse in with those two. Guy by the name of Harold Lasky. Got it real good from some sadistic bastard. You know him?"

Defiantly, I replied, "never heard of him."

"Bullshit."

Even more defiantly, I said, "you want to run me in – you know where I am."

I hung up on him and began to think about what was going on. The organization was going kill crazy. First, there was Cross's sister, then Cross and Lawrence. And they were looking for something. The office, the clothes on Lawrence and Cross, and, even B.J.'s place had been tossed. It was big. They wouldn't be going through all that if there wasn't something really big they needed to find.

I called the super and arranged to have the place cleaned. Then, I caught the IRT up to the hospital.

I almost had a heart attack when I saw B.J.'s room empty, only to turn around and see her standing in the doorway behind me. "What the hell….."

"They've discharged me. My place or yours?"

"Any place with you is fine with me, but I thought the doc said it would be a few days."

That familiar mischievous grin crept across her succulent lips and she said, "I'm a fast healer."

Fall From Apocalypse

"Let's go to your place. I have a feeling it has been have tossed again by now," I said as I began to gather up her things.

"The cops are on this big time. John was here today."

Shaking my head in disgust, I replied, "the cops. What the hell do they know? Furthermore, what the hell was John doing up here?"

"You're not still angry with him are you?"

A slight frown crept across my lips. "Why should I be angry with him. He just after my girl."

"Can't get her."

Looking down between her legs, I said, "too bad you have to wait awhile to heal down there; otherwise, I could reward you for a statement like that."

With that mischievous grin, she said, "well, maybe I will reward you this time, tiger. I still have a warm mouth that wasn't even touched by those brutes. I don't need what's between my legs to put you on cloud 9."

As she was licking her lips, I felt a slight tingle between my legs in anticipation of the delights that awaited me. Then, we went through the check-out routine, where they make certain they get their blood money before bidding you adieu. I thought to myself, just another example of an uncaring country where even competent health care is only reserved for those with the ability to pay. Why would anyone expect anything else from a society that insisted everything be part of the system that rewarded greed. Damn, I just hated what the system did to those poor souls who begged on their knees for just a small crumb from the table pf plenty that was always laid out for the privileged class.

We took a taxi to her place, said a quick hello to Mrs. Kirsh and made our way upstairs. B.J. seemed hesitant as I slid the key in. I tried to reassure her. "Nervous baby?"

"A little. Alecia was a nice kid Aaron. She didn't deserve it. She should have had a chance."

I turned the key, kicked the door open with my foot and B.J., as she looked around, said, "goddamn."

The place was ransacked from one room to another. It had been a neat and methodical search, room by room, piece by piece. The mattress had been ripped open, the sofa cut to shreds, the lamp bases busted, even the carpeting had been ripped up. Yet, all the destruction had a pattern to it that indicated professionalism.

Fall From Apocalypse

"They're looking baby. Damn, they want something and they want it bad."

"What?"

"Damned if I know, but Cross, Lawrence and Alecia must have all had access to it. That is why they are dead. And my guess is that you and I are marked now, too. We are both in danger."

There was that mischievous smile again, as she said, "does that mean you have to stick close to me?"

Smiling back, I said, "real close."

"Goodie."

She eased herself onto the floor, crossed her legs guru style and looked up at me. "I'm tired, baby."

"Want to go to dinner?"

"I sure as hell don't plan on fixing dinner here."

Thirty minutes and it was like I'd never seen her lying in the bed all battered and bruised. She walked out in a form fitting jump suit that moulded into every gorgeous curve on her long, lithe body. Her breasts seemed to surge upwards toward the heavens like two giant peeks peering into the sky.

Fall From Apocalypse

My heart began to race as I looked at her long, silky, black hair that swept across her shoulders and nestled gently on the azure suit. The midriff was cut out and each breath seemed to accentuate her smooth, flat stomach. The lower abdomen was covered just enough to prevent those beautiful dark pubic hairs that were a thicket on her love mound from peaking through.

Her legs seemed to fight the tight-fitting material, as if struggling to rip it open and flex her tight, taunt muscles that she had so often used to pull me deep inside her while we were in the throes of intense lovemaking. The material appeared to flicker in the light with each stride of the deliciously thick, muscular legs. I blurted out. "where the hell you think you are going dressed like that? You'll cause traffic accidents all over Manhattan."

"Too daring, tiger? Hey, if a girl has it, she better flaunt it while she can."

"Goddamn!"

Smiling, she replied, "now that is the kind of reaction I like."

Shaking my head, I said, "wearing a coat?"

"Now tiger, why would I do that and cover up this expensive garment?"

Fall From Apocalypse

We used B.J.'s car and it took an extra 30 minutes more than usual getting into lower Manhattan. Some idiot had forgotten to secure his load properly, and 38th Street was splattered with eggs and an overturned tractor and trailer. We had dinner at the Four Seasons, went over to a corner ice cream parlour for dessert and dropped by Sean's for a few drinks.

Sean was a jocular, chubby Irishman who was third generation American, but still spoke with a slight put-on Irish accent just to make the customers feel like they were in a real Irish bar. A graduate of Dartmouth, because his old man wanted him to be more than a bar owner, he worked on Wall Street for awhile, until he got tired of making a living off destroying people's lives with manipulations of the market. He chucked his Mercedes, big house in the Hamptons, even his expensive trophy wife, and moved back to lower Manhattan to live over the small bar that had been in his family since 1908. Ironically, he was probably richer than any of the jerks he left behind in the Hamptons, who spent all they made and then some to maintain a lifestyle that was based more on appearance than substance. Giving us the thumbs up as we walked to the bar, he said, "B.J., Aaron."

As we eased onto our stools, I smiled at him and said, "two stingers, Sean, and make them hot and heavy."

B.J. gave him that slow creeping smile. "The hot is OK, Sean, but the heavy I can do without."

"You're tops tonight B.J. Tops!"

"Thank you. I do love compliments."

Looking first at Sean, then B.J., I chortled, "stop flirting you two. Remember me, Aaron Adams?"

Sean looked at me, then B.J., then back at me and rolled his eyes. "You, I'd like to forget."

B.J. winked at Sean. "You better watch it Sean, my big tiger here can really growl."

"Ah, he's a pussy cat."

Two drinks and we were ready for two more. B.J. began to unwind and seemed to finally genuinely relax, losing the tenseness that had been subliminal, but you knew was still there. It had been tough on her, but she had seen death before, seen it several times since she had been with me. I wondered if she had seen it before then. She never talked about her life before she met me. Didn't want to for some reason. I figured her past was a bit sordid, and she just wanted to forget. Hey, the past is just that – the past. It didn't really matter to me. What she was and what she did before was immaterial. That was the problem with the country, too many people being judgmental.

Fall From Apocalypse

I smiled at her. "Baby, you look happy again."

She smiled back. "I'm with my tiger, again. Why wouldn't I be happy?"

She swivelled her stool toward me, crossed her legs and tilted her head just enough to let her hair slip down over one eye. I gave her a little wink and said, "did Alecia say anything at all that might be a clue?"

"Nothing Aaron. She mentioned Paul and said how he must have really fooled you. That's about it. We didn't have time to talk a lot."

"What about Lawrence. Any mention of him?"

"No, just Paul and something about the box." As she said the word box, a light seemed to go on in her head, as if she suddenly remembered something important.

I took that look to mean she was not sure about whether she should share the information with me or not. "The box? You want to elaborate a bit. You know something you aren't telling me."

"Oh, I wasn't paying much attention at the time. She said Paul was stupid sometimes, real stupid. He kept coming home with little boxes. He would give them to her, tell her not to open them. Then he would carefully go over them."

Even though she was talking to me, I noticed a far-away look in her eyes, as if she was also in deep thought about something else, something deep, dark and secret. She continued. "Anyway, after he would go over them, being careful not to open them until he thoroughly checked them out, he would just toss them away."

That look seemed to get deeper and further away as she continued. "That's it Aaron. Like I said, we didn't have time to talk that much."

Looking concerned, I said, "something's wrong baby. What is it?"

"Nothing. I'm just a little tired I guess." She still had that dream like quality about her. What was she thinking about that she did not want to share with me?

Sean walked over and asked if we needed another drink. B.J. consented, but I stood pat. As he removed her old drink and placed the other one down, he turned to me and said, "what about that guy diving off the Flatiron Building, Aaron? That is a good one for you. Think it was suicide or murder?"

"When this happen?"

"Oh, earlier today. I heard it on the radio around noon, I think."

"I'm already hung up, anyway. Got a real hot one to solve, and doing it for free, too."

"That's the kind of case that will put you in the poor house."

"I can't afford too many of them, Sean."

Well, maybe if you run out of cases, you can kill time by finding out whether Tornilson committed suicide or not."

The name hit me like a cool wind in the middle of a hot, humid July afternoon. "Who did you say?"

"What?"

"Who was it. Who jumped off the Flatiron?"

"Oh, ah, Tornilson. Think the first name was Mark or Mike, something like that. You know him?"

"No, no, just sounded familiar, that's all."

Sean moved down the bar at a leisurely pace, wiping the top as he went. I slipped into deep thought, and B.J. tapped my knee. "You do know him don't you, baby?"

"Yeah, yeah."

She got that determined look on her face. "Organization?"

"Small time. He was the other hood who was in your apartment."

"This thing is getting out of hand."

"You damn right, baby. And I am going to get some answers. I am off to see John Cassidy at the Silver Dollar."

"Be careful baby. There are a lot of things in this world that even the great Aaron Adams can't get to the bottom of. Sometimes, things are just the way they are, and should be left alone."

That definitely did not sound like the B.J. I knew. I told her to meet me at Frank's office in about an hour.

With that still far-away look in her eyes, she replied, " give 'um hell, Aaron."

"I've got more than hell in mind, baby. Nobody kills my old friends and then tries to take you out without suffering the consequences."

Deadly serious, she almost whispered, "there are some things that are beyond explanation, tiger. Remember that there are forces at play in this world that are beyond understanding."

Fall From Apocalypse

She stood up, turned around and started to stroll out. Looking back over her right shoulder, she said, with pouted lips, "be waiting for you."

Every bastard in the place lustfully watched as she slowly meandered out, her hips swaying provocatively side to side, making her ass cheeks jiggle just enough to make you want to touch the soft skin that lay beneath that form fitting suit. And all that was mine! She got in her car and left. Too bad I did not have the time I needed to devote to her, but as long as there was an organization, I'd always be pressed for time. Taking care of the scum who preyed on the helpless was a thankless job, but I had to do it, and I loved my job. One hour! In one hour, I would be with her again."

I paid the bill, stood on the curb and hailed a cab. As we rounded the corner of 14th Street and Broadway, I looked to my right and caught sight of B.J. in a phone booth. She seemed to be talking frantically to someone. Who was she calling that late at night?

Cassidy's bodyguards frisked me before he let me pass into the inner sanctum of John Cassidy, Mr. Big on the eastside. He was the number two or three man in the whole organization.

Without my forty-five, I felt naked, but even Aaron Adams was not going to argue with three guys with Uzi's in their hands.

Cassidy was a greasy fat bastard with an arrogant grin that he tried to use as an intimidator for those who fawned before the powerful. He did not get up from his desk, just pointed to a chair and said, "sit down, Mr. Adams."

I was not intimidated by anybody who thought they were powerful, because I lived to make the powerful realize that there was still someone left who had no fear in a world filled with sheep who cowered in supplication to those who thought they were to be exalted because of the positions they held. Government bureaucrat, politician, minister, business tycoon, royalty – they were all leeches in my book, living off the labour of the working man. I had no respect for any of them. I looked him directly in the eyes, showing no fear whatsoever. "You need to do some talking, Cassidy."

"Adam's, it's good you came, because I was going to send for you. You're the one who is going to do some talking."

Now it was time to show him what a man who wasn't cowed into subservience was capable of when confronted with evil. "You send some of your torpedoes after me asshole, and you'll wind up short of help. I talk with my mouth, or my fists, or my 45. Frankly, when talking to scumbags like you and the rest of your organization, I prefer the later two. It's a lot more fun."

Fall From Apocalypse

Cassidy nodded at the flunky who ushered me in. "Leave us alone Drew. Mr. Adams and I have some personal matters to talk over."

"Yes, sir."

He gave me a determined look. "I want it Adams. You understand!"

"Just what is it you want?"

Shaking his head slightly and pursing his lips for effect, he said, "you know, Adams. And you damn well better deliver. You think an awful lot of your secretary don't you? Now, I am sure you don't want anything to happen to her."

"No I wouldn't Cassidy. And if anything does, I'll come back here personally to tear your eye balls out. So, don't try to intimidate me. You scare a lot of people with your terror tactics, but Aaron Adams doesn't scare so easily. You lay one grimy little hand on B.J. again, and I'm liable to destroy the whole organization. You ain't never seen me really angry. What I did to your boys in the past doesn't even come close to what I am capable of doing."

"I want the goddamn box, Adams, right now."

"Box? You son-of-a-bitch; I don't know what you are talking about."

"I'm going to kill you Adams, but first I am going to torture you until you tell me where it is, and then you will beg me to kill you to alleviate your pain. If you give me what I want now, you can avoid the absolute worst pain any human being could suffer. The box, you bastard, the box!"

That was it. I was going to get nothing out of him. I snapped. I dived over the desk and knocked the bastard out of his high-priced leather chair. The bodyguards bolted through the door, Uzis in hand. I stood Cassidy up as a shield, reached for the letter opener on the desk and put it to his neck. They all grimaced as I peered around with a smile. "Pull the triggers assholes, or drop 'um if you don't want this slimy bastard's guts all over the floor."

Cassidy was breathing like a locomotive climbing a steep grade. Screaming, he said, "goddamn boys, do what he says. Do what he says."

Still smiling, I said, "that's nice boys. Put the Uzis down and place my 45 on the table."

I reached out and retrieved my old friend from the desk. I hit Cassidy in the back of the head with it and he crumbled to the floor. Drew started toward me, but he stopped about three feet away when he met some hot lead from my baby."

Fall From Apocalypse

The rest of them were trembling with fear. "OK boys, we've had our fun now. Let's get down to some serious business. I am really disappointed in your hospitality. I am sure your mothers taught you better than that. I am going to have to punish you."

The three torpedoes were really shaking now. They had come up against someone who was capable of more cruelty than they were. I smiled at them and squeezed off a round. One of them, gripping his left shoulder where a bullet had made a nice little hole, fell to the floor wreathing in agony.

Cassidy, now coming to, stuttered, "uh, uh, Adams, you, you can't kill us in cold blood."

I bent over and picked up one of the Uzis. Still smiling, I really let them know how wrong they were. "You're wrong Cassidy. I can and I am."

"Adams…………."

First, I turned on the three bodyguards still standing. I cut loose with a volley of shots that threw them back against the wall and reeling to the floor. Then I turned to the one I had shot who was still on the floor. What the hell, I thought. Why waste bullets. The things were too expensive to waste on a two-bit hood like Drew. I took the butt of my gun and buried it in his forehead.

While this was happening, Cassidy was crawling toward the window. What did he want – a little fresh air? I yelled, "stop where you are Cassidy."

He stopped, rolled over on his back and started to plead for mercy. I ignored the whimpering from him and Drew both, grabbed a chair and had a seat. Damn, I thought, killing is real hard work when you really put your heart and soul into it.

Listening to them whimpering and pleading, I just sat and enjoyed having the abusers be abused for a change. Cassidy looked up at me, his eyes pleading for mercy. "Don't worry Cassidy. I haven't forgotten you."

Now he was really scared. "Adams, Adams, please, please. I beg you. I beg you."

I got up, went over to him and said, "don't waste your breath, asshole."

I cut lose with a mighty kick and broke ribs as I buried my foot in his chest. Then I picked up a chair, shoved the leg in his mouth and sat down for a coffee break. Damn, there was no coffee!

Cassidy kept mumbling something, so I pulled the chair leg out of his mouth and buried my shoe heel in his fat face. The bastard had just about had it. It looked like the fun was over, when a brilliant idea hit me.

J. Wayne Frye

Fall From Apocalypse

I observed two large curtain rods on the window and decided to do some interior decorating. I removed one of the rods, went over to Cassidy, propped him up and shoved the rod all the way through his neck. Then I picked the fat tub of lard up, carried him over to the window like a skewered pig and hung him up like a curtain. I thought I might have a new career as an interior decorator, using hoods for curtains. He was still breathing, but only slightly conscious. I looked up at him and said, "goodnight Cassidy. Damn man, you shouldn't hang around places like this."

Drew thought he was getting his next, but I just looked down and smiled at him. "I'm letting you live Drew, so you can tell the big boys that Aaron Adams is coming, and they ain't none of 'um safe. You let them know."

As I meandered towards the door, I began singing, "mine eyes have seen the glory of the coming of ...."

Once outside, I took in a big breath of fresh air, then thought about what Cassidy was concerned with – the box. What was it about the box?

CHAPTER 5
BABY, NOW YOU'RE SUPERCHARGED

B.J. and I had worked with Frank Vunovich on several cases. He was a private eye from the old school, but he was damn adaptable to the modern school. Sixty-two years old, and he was still packing a rod, stilling mingling with the so-called low-lives, still peeping through windows, still earning his bread by prying into people's lives. B.J. and I often dropped by his combination office-apartment for a night-cap. I thought he was a little gaga over her. I knew he was. Who wasn't.

It was an old renovated brownstone off 68th. It was a little too far to walk, so I hailed a cab. After sweeping through caution lights and taking several turns on two wheels, the guy who was better suited to driving NASCAR than a cab, pulled up alongside B.J.'s Volkswagen. I paid the fare and suggested to that driver that his next trip should be on the Indianapolis Speedway. He gave me a big grin, thanked me for the tip and spun out like he was at starting Le Mans.

I looked up at the fifth floor of the building and noticed Frank had every light in his place on. Hell, with the enemies he had made over the years, he probably not only slept with the lights on but old newspapers crumbled up around his bed to make sure no one was able to sneak up on him when he was sleeping.

Fall From Apocalypse

It wasn't an elevator, just an old fashioned open lift. It took a good five minutes to go up five floors, but the trip gave me time to straighten my tie and brush some of the wrinkles out of my suit.

Before I stepped out of the lift, I pulled out the 45. One look at the place and I knew something was amiss. The air was thick and heavy with the smell of cordite. Someone had fired a weapon.

I did not bother to knock at the door, just placed my foot against it and gave a mighty kick. There was no need to hit the floor. The action was over. One look told me that.

The damn place looked like Miami after Hurricane Camille went through. There was nothing left standing. Even the walls had been ripped open.

There was blood leading from one corner of the office to behind the overturned desk. A groan from behind the desk told me that I wasn't alone.

Frankie was alright, but the size of the hole in his side explained the smell of gun powder. Some son-of-a-bitch was hawking a sawed-off shotgun.

He was still breathing, slowly but rhythmically. His outstretched hand and the direction it was facing indicated he had been trying to reach the telephone.

I crawled over the debris and dialled the newly instituted number for emergencies, 911. His eyelids opened slowly and he stared up at me with glazed eyes. I encouragingly said, "stick with it Frankie. Stick with it. Ambulance is on the way. "

He mumbled, "I'll make it. But they got B.J. They got B.J. I heard it. I heard it."

"Heard what?"

"Heard where they are taking her. They called a woman after, after…." His voice trailed off, but he struggled to continue. "After that bastard drilled me."

"You have any idea who they called?"

"Sure, I heard B.J. tell them after the call. She said to the guy who called, so, Cindy Phillips is a plant, uh?"

That was B.J. for you. She knew Frankie was conscious and would hear her say Cindy's name. Then, he would tell me. Cindy Phillips was a friend of B.J.'s who had more than once thrown a pass my way. She lived in the apartment next to B.J.'s. She had been planted there by the organization to keep tabs on her, and thereby, also on me. But why had they called her after shooting Frankie and abducting B.J.? What were they up to? It was definitely something nefarious.

Fall From Apocalypse

"Hang on Frankie. Hang on. The ambulance will be here soon. I have to go over to Cindy's and find out where they have taken B.J."

He was too weak to talk. He just motioned with his index finger for me to go. I left him lying in a pool of blood, but he would make it. He was tough enough to take it in the gut and walk away, only living for the pleasure of getting the bastard who drilled him.

I caught the uptown express and began to anticipate my meeting with Cindy on the way up. She was about to come face-to-face with the devil. She was going to pay for her treachery, female or not. You mess with me, that is one thing. You mess with B.J., that is another. Nobody, but nobody would be allowed to mess with her.

I slipped up the back way in order to avoid Mrs. Kirsh. Cindy was a bit reluctant to let me in, but when I told her that I had come to take her up on that last offer of a romp in paradise, she seemed to think I knew nothing about what had happened to B.J. Or was she just toying with me until the goon squad arrived, or she got me in a compromising position where she could take me out when my guard was down.

She headed toward the bar and pulled the one string on her gown, flipped her shoulder and it fell to the floor as she stepped out of it.

Fall From Apocalypse

Her, round, magnificent ass was supposed to divert my attention from the pills she dropped in my drink, but I'd been that route one time too many not to pick up on a Mickey-Finn.

She turned toward me, sauntered my way exposing that magnificent split between her legs that, no doubt, made men go wild with desire. With drinks in each hand, she was smiling, thinking to herself that she had me, and was about to eliminate me with ease. "I'll just take these to the bedroom where we can relax better."

I gave her a sinister smile. "Coming, Cindy."

"You'd better come." She turned on the last word and gave me the real enticement routine by taking long strides to stretch the muscles of her butt and expose the hairs between the back of her luscious thighs. I waited for her to disappear into the bedroom, and then I heard, "hurry up darling. I need something big and juicy to nibble on. I am really hungry for some protein. I love to coat my throat with protein. It makes it feel so good."

I began to remove my coat as I made my way toward the bedroom. I got to the door, and she was sprawled out on the bed, legs spread wide with her fingers working furiously between them manipulating her mound of desire in anticipation of some intense lovemaking before I passed out. She shouted, "give it to me baby. I need it now."

Smirking now, I replied, "you may have to wait."

Nervously she said, "what is it, Aaron?"

I looked down at her and tossed the drink, glass and all, against the wall. "You ever heard of Mark Tornilson or Harold Laskey?"

There was a slight tremble in her voice. "No, I don't think so."

I moved closer. She squirmed a little, pulled her index finger out of her love mound and licked her lips, "Why?"

I moved closer. "They were hoods."

"So?"

I moved closer. "They were tied up in something big. Something real big. Something about a box. Something that has caused a lot of untimely deaths. Something the syndicate, the organization wants desperately."

I moved closer. "Desperate enough to kill again and again for it. You've heard of the syndicate baby. The organization. Those who make a career out of crime, only they aren't always as subtle as the corporations or the government. They are more open about their thievery."

I moved closer, as she said, "syndicate, organization? What is wrong with you? You gone crazy?" She eased up in a sitting position.

I moved closer, edging my way to the top of the bed. "They've got B.J., Cindy, and you know I will do whatever it takes to get her back. You don't want to see how far I will go to get the information."

"God. Oh, God!"

"God's not going to help you Cindy. You and I both know there is no God. But there is a devil, and he has come calling. It's me. Where the hell is B.J.?"

"Please, Aaron, Please! They suckered me in. Honest to God, they suckered me in! I got a place up here, gave up hooking, and they laid it on the line."

I wasn't buying it. "Bullshit! You've never done any street walking. Class, baby, class. One of the big boys has you as a mistress, put you in here to keep an eye out for me and a possible set-up. Then Cross's sister walks into the picture. You know the organization wants Paul, so you figure to give them his sister."

She was beginning to tremble uncontrollably, "Aaron, Aaron!"

Fall From Apocalypse

I flattened my fist as if was going to backhand her across the face. She began to whimper. "You're going to give me some answers, goddamn it. You hear me, bitch?"

"Ask all you want you son-of-bitch. You're not getting noting out of me. You hear? Nothing, I tell you," she said as she shook her head wildly.

"The name's Adam's baby, Aaron Adams, the one who can kill and never regret. You know, the one who dumped Fluke Williams, well, what was left of him anyway, in the trashcan. The one who battered the hell out of Lasky. Then, there's the ones the organization doesn't even know about. The ones they figure are too gory for even me to commit. Hey, I've killed more than they'll ever be able to count, and you know what? I enjoyed it immensely. You remember the one they found on the Westside a few years ago. The one with her nipples pinched off with a pair of pliers, and a steel rod jammed up her ass so far it came out her chest. That was me, baby. Me! An Adam's special." It was mostly lies, but it was scaring the hell out of her.

"You wouldn't. The organization will know, They'll know." She was beginning to shake frantically.

"Yeah, baby. They'll know. I want them to know who did it, but you'll still be dead."

"Please, please."

"Who hired you?"

"No, no!"

"Where's B.J.?"

"Please, Aaron! Please. You can't do this. You can't!" She was getting hysterical.

"Who is your go between, then? Give me that, and I'll get it out of him where B.J. is."

She began to cry, shake her head, breath more quickly. Her eyes were pleading.

She started to scream, so I put my hand over her mouth and tilted her head upward. I gave her the death smile. "Hey, baby, I enjoy this. You're part of the organization. And anybody who is part of the organization I love to torment. I love to give them some of what they dish out. The army trained me to kill, but the good old USA also taught me how to torture. Oh, they keep it a secret, but we are no better than any of those third world countries we are always condemning. Only difference is, we never leave any witnesses to our torture. I learned a lot, and I learned it good. I am a master baby, a real master. It has been awhile, I may be a little rusty, but it is just like riding a bicycle. It'll all come back."

Fall From Apocalypse

I reached over on her night stand and picked up a silk stocking. I tied it around her neck. "Now you scream baby, and I'll snap every bone in your neck."

She took a deep breath and tried to control her fear. I bent over a little closer and whispered in her ear. "Give me the answers."

"I can't! Oh God, I can't!"

Very slowly and quietly I said, "you can. You can."

"Please. Please."

I eased off the stocking, reached behind the bed with my left hand and pulled out the lamp switch. I picked her up by the mid-section and tied the sheet around her waist. I pulled the sheet snug and tied the lose end to the bed post.

I was really smiling now. "Baby, I am glad you want to do this the hard way. Hell, I'd miss a lot of fun if you just told me now."

I pulled out my pocket knife. She began to squirm. I cut the wire off near the base of the lamp, frayed the rubber back at the end to expose the copper wire and put the plug back into the wall. Never letting my smile fade, I said, "You're getting curious aren't you, baby?

Fall From Apocalypse

Her eyes were about to pop out of their sockets, as I went into the bathroom and came out with her douche syringe. I picked up the two flayed ends and wrapped them around the syringe, being careful not to touch the two copper wires and shock myself. The sinister smile was still there and her eyes kept getting bigger and bigger. Pleading she said, "Aaron, Aaron, what…."

Before she could finish, I tied the nylon stocking around her mouth and went to work. I spread her legs and glided the syringe into her vagina nice and easy. The electric current began to generate some real excitement. Hell, it was the best screw she had ever had – at least the most shocking, anyway.

"Are you ready to talk now, baby?" I said as I eased off the gag.

She desperately shook her head. "You son-of-bitch. You mother…."

Before she could get it out, I wrapped the gag around her again and whispered, "baby, it's gong to get worse."

She started to scream, but I pulled out the syringe and gave her gums an electric cleaning. Hell, she would be the only girl in town with battery-powered gums. I grinned long and hard as my eyes moved methodically toward her breasts.

J. Wayne Frye

Fall From Apocalypse

She knew what was coming. She pleaded with her eyes and rather than screaming, she just whispered, "no, no."

I gave her nipples an electric charge. Hell, they looked kind of run down anyway. She wanted to scream like a locomotive coming around a curve, but she couldn't. The fear was so intense, all she could do was shake her head from side to side. I jammed the syringe in her belly button.

"I'll talk. I'll talk. Oh God, I'll talk."

In a low voice with no inflection whatsoever, I said, "I kind of thought you would."

Turning off the intensity of my gaze and smile, I tried to be a bit more comforting. "Just tell me about B.J., first. Where is she?"

She is at Howard Frailey's place. 32-14 60th Street in Queens, near Forest Hills. They took her there to do just what you did to me. Make her tell them where she is hiding the box."

"The box. What they hell is this box everybody is talking about?"

"Don't know, honest. I don't know except it is supposed to be a little smaller than a cigar box. The organization has been after it for years, ever since it was smuggled into the country. They have never been able to find it, though. Never."

"So, the organization thinks B.J. has it since she was with Cross's sister?"

She took a few quick breaths before replying. "Partly, see, they first thought that was the only connection, then an operative in Washington let them know that B.J. had access to the box years ago, somewhere in Tibet, when she worked for the CIA."

B.J.'s past was now slapping me in the face. Goddamn, a CIA operative. That is why she never shared any information about her past. At Sean's, she had that look – that look of recognition about the box. It was written all over her face, only I didn't know it at the time. While she was sitting at the bar, she had realized that the box Alecia Cross has mentioned was the same box she had come across years before. But why hadn't she told me? And what the hell made the box so important? And who was she calling that night from the phone booth, away from my prying eyes?

Cindy Phillips was still scared. She couldn't take her eyes off me. "Lawrence and Cross, why were they taken out?"

"Cross was working with the organization, but he got caught up in a smuggling operation. They didn't take care of him then. Just booted him out."

Fall From Apocalypse

The fear was still there, but she continued with her story. "The organization didn't know he knew they were looking for the box. Anyway, Cross got obsessed with getting back at the organization. Figured getting the box would really make them pay, but big. Seems this guy Lawrence was just an innocent bystander. Cross got his hands on the box, the one the organization wanted, only he passed it on to Lawrence for safe-keeping, or so the organization figured, anyway. Only neither of them had it."

"And Alecia Cross?"

"I knew she was Cross's sister. The organization was looking for Paul. I figured she might know."

"So, you set her and B.J. up?"

"Please, no. Never."

"Who is your contact?"

"Please…."

"Don't make me ask you again."

Shaking her head from side to side, she knew that she had no choice. I was a man who would not be trifled with. I had too much on the line. "I work through Cassidy. John Cassidy, only he's not around anymore is he, Aaron?"

"You damn right he's not. Who did he answer to?"

"What the hell. I'm dead either way. If you don't take care of me, they will."

I looked out her bedroom window and saw a car pull up. You could recognize they were hoods by the expensive suits they were wearing and their arrogant bearing. Hell, they looked like bankers, only these bankers were bit more honest. They did their killing in the open, rather than in the corporate board rooms where the barons of greed used nefarious means to rob, steal and kill the hopes and dreams of one American after another.

Knowing I only had a few seconds until they got up to her apartment, I said, "hey baby, you might get lucky. There won't be any evidence you told me anything. I'll make it look like you resisted real good. So, who else is in the chain of command?"

"Howard Frailey. That's it. Frailey is as high as I ever went, but I know Frailey answers to a mayor of a small town in Connecticut, and that Frailey is also accountable to some dentist in Manhattan. Don't know the dentist's name, just know he is a big shot. That's all."

Knowing my time was running out, I said, "thanks Cindy, I'll fix you up for the boys."

Fall From Apocalypse

"What you mean?"

"Four torpedoes are on their way to rescue you."

She couldn't believe she was so close to being rescued before she spilled her guts. She looked up at me with eyes that could pierce through a steel door. I was pressed for time and had to hurry. Smiling, I tied secured her hands with the sheet and pulled the frayed ends of the cord further apart. I put one up her vagina and jammed the other in her butt. She was squirming from the shock, and I said as I bent down and headed out the window for the fire escape, "the boys will really think you said nothing baby from the looks of you. Before they find out your spilled your guts get out of town fast."

As I headed down the stairs, I couldn't helped but look back, give her the big smile and say, "baby, now you're super charged."

CHAPTER 6
I HAD A DENTAL APPOINTMENT

Frailey lived in an upscale Long Island neighbourhood where he was just another of the blood suckers who lived the good-life off what they stole from the working men and women who really did all the work in the country. He belonged right there with the stock brokers, the hedge fund managers, the venture capitalists, the bankers – all those who sucked the life out of capitalism and had the government in the palms of their hands. These were the people who ridiculed and attacked the middle class and poor as leeches, when it was they who were the real leeches in a society that had no respect for those who toiled in the factories and offices of despair in service to these monoliths of crony capitalism and organized crime.

I parked B.J.'s car a few hundred feet away from Frailey's house. I figured B.J. was safe for awhile as they would probably not do anything to her there. They would have to leave for the kill. Frailey definitely wouldn't do anything in his nice suburban home. Hell, he'd order the kill and probably be sitting in church Sunday morning with his family. At 4:00 AM in the morning, it was the only house in the neighbourhood with the lights on. Just as I was about to get out of the car and creep up toward the house, two muscle guys walked out the front entrance, got into a light coloured sedan and drove off.

Fall From Apocalypse

It was time to make my move. With only two other cars in the driveway, the odds were Frailey was alone. I carefully worked my way to the living room window, eased down on all fours and peered into the living room. Frailey was all by himself, talking on the phone. Who the hell was he talking to at 4:00 AM?

There was no doubt Cindy had either lied or just been wrong. B.J. was not there. I knew it.

I thought a four o'clock phone call might be interesting, so I eased up close to the window and listened intently. I had no idea what was being said on the other end, but the way Frailey was constantly saying "yes sir," it was obvious it was one of his organization superiors. Hell, he sounded like some damn enlisted army man who was always being forced to kiss officer ass. The organization and the army were no different. They both exploited people and made their members servants to the elite. The poor slobs in the army were sent off to foreign lands and told they were defending freedom. The only thing they were defending was the powerful business interests that saw profits in war. They had been fed a steady diet of propaganda since they were kids, brought up standing dutifully every morning in school pledging allegiance to an ideal that didn't even exist, so they could be prepped as cannon fodder for the powerful interests that wanted to make the world safe for American corporate power.

Fall From Apocalypse

Hell, Vietnam was an obscene abomination of wanton carnage. Why send kids over there to die, so America could control the lives of people who just wanted to be left alone to grow a little rice and take care of their families, free of corporations. The organization and the army, they were no different, even their methods were pretty much the same. Only the organization was a bit more subtle with their killing. They didn't rain terror down from 80,000 feet with thousand pound incendiary bombs or napalm that destroyed everything in sight.

Frailey lit a cigarette, sit down and propped his feet up on the coffee table as he continued talking. "Yes sir, I know. My son, the little bastard, I gave him strict orders to keep his mouth shut. You don't have to worry about him. He is hung up on the juice, but he's a damn good enforcer. He's in with the east-side bunch now, but he'll grow up. Anyway, he knows the ropes. He knows where the boys took Holden. He'll be home before long and give me the details on what happened. I figured it would be better to turn her over to the east-side bunch and let them work it out of her. That way, I keep her away from me, and there is no tie-in with the organization. My boy, when she spills the information will pick up the box and bring it to me. He knows not to open it. The gang is tough, plenty tough, and they will scare the hell out of her. Believe me, she will talk. Then, after she talks, they will have some fun with her, every one of them. Then, they'll dump the body and we are not connected in any way."

I had what I wanted. B.J. was with a bunch of backstreet hoods, but where could I find them? I would take care of them, but first I was going to take care of Frailey.

He "yes sired" a few more times and hung up by saying, "good-bye Dr. Malick." O.K., now I had them both. No problem finding Malick, I thought. He'd be listed in the Manhattan phone directory under dentists. He was the son-of-a-bitch Cindy Phillips had heard about. He'd tell me where to find B.J.

I'd take care of Malick. Take damn good care of him, but Frailey was first. About he time he turned-off the living room lights, I rang the front doorbell. He opened up the little peephole and swivelled his eyeball from side to side, but couldn't see me as I stepped to one side and leaned against the house.

He opened the door and stupidly stepped onto the porch. I moved in front of him and let out with a grin.

When in the course of human events it becomes necessary to kill a son-of-a-bitch, you can sure as hell count on Aaron Adams to get the job done. I couldn't wait to see Frailey squirm. I slapped hell out of his face with the barrel of my forty-five. The left side of his face caved in like an over-ripe watermelon that had just rolled off a kitchen table onto a tile floor. The bastard fell through a cedar bush and lay their whimpering like a baby.

I picked up a nearby water hose, slid it under his right leg and tied a knot in it so tight his bones popped. I dragged the son-of-a-bitch through the shrubbery toward the driveway, smiling every bit of the way while he was screaming for me to stop.

Hell, I'd stop alright, when he knew what it was like to deal with the wrath of Aaron Adams. I had not uttered one word when I realized it was time he knew his tormentor. Without stopping, I looked over my should and said two words. "Aaron Adams!"

It was like a damn shockwave. He let out with one long, resounding scream that brought lights on all over the neighbourhood. His wife came to the front door with her hair in curlers and began to scream like a banshee. I reached inside the coat, brought out the forty-five, shot out the porch light, and she ran back inside.

I continued down the driveway toward the garage, pulling Frailey behind me. The hose began to loosen on his leg, so I bent over to tighten it and noticed a gigantic power mower beside the garage. I picked up the hose and tried to pull him a little further, but it was no use, so I just left the bastard there crying like a baby.

The mower started with the first pull. It was a powerful bastard. Frailey turned on his side and stared at me as he tried to get to his feet.

Pushing the mower forward, I stopped about three feet from Frailey and gave him the big smile with all the teeth showing. The hum of the mower rang through my head like a symphony, and the symbols kept clanking away until I felt that I was right up there on stage, conducting a great orchestra.

The poor slob did not know what I had in mind. I guess it was more frightening for him not knowing what to expect. By the time I mowed off his left arm at the elbow, he knew what I had in mind. Damn, he was going to get a close cut. I stared down and said, "B.J., you mess with her, you pay bastard."

The symphony went wild in my head, and I got lost in the tempo of the music. When the driveway was painted red and my clothes were splattered with bits of bone and flesh, I decided to stop mowing. Hell, I thought, I never knew mowing could be so much fun. I kind of hated to leave, but what the hell. I had mowed the son-of-a-bitch up, and I sure as hell wasn't going to mow his grass for him. This was a calling card that the organization would remember for a very long time.

I walked down the driveway and looked back at the mower. It was still running. What the hell, some of his neighbours might come over and trim Frailey around the edges. That was if they could find any edges to trim. The sounds of sirens in the distance blended nicely with the hum of the mower. Yeah, I was in a rich neighbourhood, so the cops would be hauling ass to serve the rich and powerful while crime in the ghetto was being ignored.

I quickly walked back to the car, and before getting in, took the heel of my right foot and kicked the light over the licence plate out to obscure the number. The lights were beginning to come on all around me, and frantic voices were beginning to filter my way.

I cruised down the street slow and easy, and waved as a patrol car passed me in the opposite direction. When the lights disappeared from my rear view mirror, I slammed on the accelerator and hit the freeway back to the city. It was now almost 5:00 AM, and the clock was ticking on B.J. I had to find her soon, before they took her out. She was tough, and would hold out as long as she could, knowing I would be looking for her. I needed to go home, shower, change clothes and brush my teeth. I had a dental appointment.

CHAPTER 7
BEFORE I CALMED DOWN

It was a damn fine morning, damn fine. I was almost there, almost had B.J. in my arms again. Just a few more corpses and the two of us would be back together. When it came to the organization, I loved piling up corpses. The only thing better would be putting all the country's CEO's into a giant pile, pouring some gas over them and incinerating their asses until the last vestige of their greed was scattered in the wind to never more infest humanity. Between the organization and corporations, life in America had been reduced to nothing more than a struggle by the middle class and poor to just survive one more day in a system of financial bondage. People thought they were free, but they were too stupid to realize that as long as you depended on a corporation for your job and the food you put on your table, there was no freedom. Freedom had ended the minute people left the farm and turned to their corporate masters to supply them with the necessities of life. The only ones free were the greedy one percent who sat at the top, knowing that they controlled the government and thereby, the people. Wealth and power always flowed to those at the top, while the rest toiled in misery for just a scrap from the table of plenty. Well, Aaron Adams never played their game. I had foolishly served my country in a war of conquest, and I had finally seen through the veil of deceit.

Well, Dr. Malick was a part of that one percent, and he was about to meet one of the 99% who would not bow in supplication to those who thought they were part of the privileged class. I walked into his office like I owned the joint. The damn organization bitch who sat out front smiled at first, but I wiped it away quickly by saying, "where's Malick. I know this office is a front, so don't give me any shit. Just tell me where Malick is."

"He's, he's inside."

Grabbing her by the arm and pulling her with me, I said, "let's go baby. You may enjoy watching me beat hell out of your employer."

I didn't bother to knock. I just kicked the door open and went in like the USA invading another helpless country to bring it democracy with bullets and bombs. Malick was standing beside the dental chair that probably hadn't had a patient in it for years. Seeing I meant business, he reached down for a prong that was, no doubt, a good prop for the times when he was visited by police. He could play at being a dentist, even though he had no patients.

The sexy little blond haired bitch started shouting obscenities, so I gave her a backhand across the face, and she crumbled in silence to the floor. She would be quiet for awhile.

Fall From Apocalypse

Malick tried to get me with the dental prong, but he only got a mouth full of fist for the effort. I picked up the bastard and deposited him in the dental chair. Hell, I though I might pull a few teeth. I ripped off his white jacket, tore it apart and tied the son-of-a-bitch down with it.

As he breathed heavily, I leaned in real close. "Malick, you and the organization sent two torpedoes after me in the last two years. That was your first mistake, but I must admit that I really enjoyed doing Fluke Williams. You bastards should know by now that I am not afraid of the organization. But then you bastards really made a big mistake when you went after B.J. The son-of-bitch who raped her is probably still trying to scrape up his guts. But they all had it easy compared to what you are going to get. It's time you boys finally learned your lesson. Fucking with me is one thing, but fucking with B.J. is another."

"Adams, please, please…."

I picked up one of the V-shaped prongs off the tray and pried his mouth open so wide that his jaw bones popped. He would be quiet now.

The little bitch tried to get up and run, but it was like a turtle trying to outrun a jaguar. I ripped away her dress and she was completely nude under it, not even any panties. I shoved her against the wall, as Malick squirmed in the chair.

I pulled her over to Malick and said, "so, you think humping this guy will get you ahead in life. Baby, this guy is finished. He can die quick, or he can die slow. It depends on how fast he tells me what I want to know. Now, I don't enjoy hurting women, but, if necessary, to get what I want, I will hurt you. You give me any trouble, and I can kill you, too. I don't want to, but I will."

I had no intention of killing her, but she didn't know that, and she had seen what I did to Malick. She shook her head and said, "I'll, I'll be quiet. I'll be quiet."

I pushed her down in a chair to the left of Malick and said, "you move baby, and you'll never move again."

She was too scared to talk, she just shook her head up and down. I winked at her and turned to Malick. "Kind of sexy ain't she?"

The horror was in his eyes. He knew that intense pain was about to come his way.

Again, I leaned in close. "Malick, the organization is really big, but nothing is too big for me, not even the U.S. government. If you believe in God, you better start praying, because you are about to meet your maker. Now, you can meet him quick, with relatively no pain, or we can let me enjoy myself. It's your choice."

Fall From Apocalypse

I thought back to the times in the army when I had been taught how to torture the enemy. The American public was told America didn't torture, and they actually believed it. Yeah, and America didn't commit atrocities either. Anyone who wanted to study a little history could find out the truth, but that took an effort, and the public was so gullible they actually swallowed the propaganda without question. Americans were the most brainwashed people in the world, not the communists. Just ask the American Indians if the United States tortured.

Well, Dr. Malick was going to have to make a choice. He could talk and save himself some pain, or he could make me get the information the hard way. Fortunately, he chose the latter.

Through the prongs he shouted, "I'm not telling you shit."

"Malick, I'm glad you said that. I'd miss a lot of fun. You know, once when I worked with army intelligence, I was in Austria on a mission to assassinate a Russian courier. He had killed one of our operatives, really tortured him bad, so they sent me over to take him out in a way that would leave a message the Russians would never forget. He lived for four days, mostly skinned alive. I sat there and watched him beg for death, but I just smiled. When they found him, he was still alive. Mercifully, they put him out of his intense misery.

You see Malick, I love doing this."

I didn't bother to close the prongs when I pulled them out of his mouth. They got caught up in some teeth, but Dr. Adams, with a little twisting and pulling finally got the job done. Maybe I should have been a dentist rather than a detective.

Almost whispering, I said, "where is she, asshole?"

He spat blood in my face and shouted, "fuck you."

I picked up the high speed drill. Hell, I felt like a kid with a new toy. The hum and buzz of the motor sent goose pimples up and down my spine. Again I whispered, "where is she?"

I gave him the death smile that begins way down deep in the pit of the stomach and works it way ever so slowly up to the lips, which, at first just part mildly, then rapidly open to reveal grinning, gleaming white teeth. I couldn't resist laughing out loud. He knew I was moving in for the real torture.

The naked woman buried her hands in her head, almost sobbing. I ask one more time, "where is she?"

"Never. I'll never tell!"

Fall From Apocalypse

I slid the drill over his torn and lacerated lips, letting the hum of the motor play a symphony for his horror-filled mind. Suddenly, without warning, I went to work. I drilled what was left of his front teeth. Then went to work on the big babies in the back. After awhile, I got tired, because they were so hard to reach, and I could hardly see them for all the blood and debris in his mouth.

The woman through tears cried out, "please, please tell him. If you don't, I will."

OK, that was it, I didn't need Malick any more. She knew. She knew."

I gripped his right jaw between my index finger and thumb. Then, I cut the jaw open with a smooth, straight flow of the drill. Now, I could see all his teeth.

The bastard was about to pass out, but he was just conscious enough to feel my final performance on his teeth. I shoved the drill in his gums and began to sing "Give Me That Old Time Religion." The drill hit bone and I had to yank it out. That was when the woman said, "I'm telling him. I'm telling him. Bumpy Morgan's place is where he is supposed to meet the guy who has her. The Eastside boys turned her over to a special operative they brought in just to handle this. Don't hurt him any more, please. Just kill him and get it over with."

Damn, I'd been drilling all morning, broke a bit and still hadn't struck oil, but I stuck something better. I never heard of Bumpy Morgan, so I turned and asked the girl where it was.

"It is in the Bowery, 114 Bowery Street."

Malick was slowly dying. He looked like he had been in a contest with a thrashing machine and lost. I turned to the crying woman and said, "baby, when the big boys get here, tell them to get a good look at Malick, because if they mess with B.J., the whole organization is going to look like this, courtesy of Aaron Adams.

I turned and headed out the door. Aaron Adams was sky-high and the gravediggers were going to draw plenty of overtime before I calmed down.

CHAPTER 8
TOMORROW WOULD BE
THE DAY OF THE GUN

I had been in the Bowery enough to know that it was just a microcosm of all that was wrong with America. This was the place where the used up people were dumped. While the bankers, the wizards of Wall Street, the politicians and the organization thugs of despair all lived the high life, those who had been ground up by the machinery of capitalism came to the dens of inequity to crawl in squalor and live out their lives in quiet desperation, uncared for by a society that hypocritically held itself up as a beacon of hope to the world. These were the examples of the cruelty of a system based on greed. The country was filled with these monuments to despair promulgated by a society where all the good things flowed to those at the top and the vast majority lived in desperation and fear of what the next day would bring as they toiled in the factories, the offices and fields of misery that trapped them in an endless cycle of servitude. And the organization was a part of what made this the rule, rather than the exception. Between the government and the organization, the common man had no hope of pulling himself up from the wretchedness and woe that was the lot of those who were used by the system of evil that trapped all but a few in a life of desperation. The government was the worst offender, but the organization was a close second.

Fall From Apocalypse

The junkies, the prostitutes, the hungry, the lame of body and spirit were the forgotten ones in a society that had no heart and no soul. They were all forgotten by those with the power to change things, but could never muster the will and courage to do the right thing. Politicians made promises, but promises did not fill empty bellies, nor did they fill the empty spirits of those in despair who simply needed a hand up, rather than the backhand of contempt. Well, I could fill bellies, fill organization bellies with lead from my forty-five. I'd fill them so full of lead that they would need a dump truck for a hearse to compensate for the extra weight.

I stopped at a phone booth and called John Havoc to see if he had any information on Bumpy Morgan, but he was not in. I ambled down the street toward Bumpy's. It was a dilapidated building, with boarded up windows that had Bumpy's scrawled in bright read paint across the plywood.

A moderately tall, well-built but dirty-looking man smiled at me with what was left of his teeth from behind a pock-marked counter and said, "well, I was expecting you. Aaron Adams, no doubt."

Somewhat surprised at his friendliness, I replied, "that's right. I understand you might be a man who could help me."

Fall From Apocalypse

Still smiling, he said, "I might be able to help. Words out that your good-looking secretary has been swiped. Maybe you ought to keep your nose outta other people's business and things like that wouldn't happen." His voice sounded strangely familiar. Him, I didn't know, but the voice. The voice I had heard before. I knew the voice.

"Other people's business is my business."

"Well, this time, apparently, you have picked the wrong people to snoop on, Mr. Adams."

"That may be right, but I will get B.J. back. I assure you of that."

"I have good sources, Mr. Adams, very good sources. I do think that can be arranged."

Getting tired of the banter, I cut to the chase. "Well, I got a few bills for you, if you can put me on the right trail."

"Money ain't no good to a dead man, Mr. Adams. Word is out about this here box that the big boys is looking for, and that you the daddy who holds the key."

"So why B.J.? Why not me?"

"Insurance daddy, insurance. Everybody knows you ain't gonna talk, but to save her – well?"

"The box, the goddamn box! Suppose I did have the box, could you set up a meet?"

"Ain't saying Adams. I might and I might not."

I moved in close enough to notice that underneath his coat, he was obviously packing a rod. Looking into his eyes, they seemed familiar. His clothing was old and tattered, but it looked as if it had been ripped and torn in a methodical way. "Bumpy, I'm going after the bastards who have her. Now, if they want to play rough, that's fine, but tell them I have played the game before. If they want a sample of what I am capable of, just have them visit Dr. Malick's office. You cut that lose on the grapevine."

There was something strange about his missing teeth. I couldn't put my finger on it, but there was something really familiar and weird about the guy.

"Adams, this here box, you got it?"

His inquisitiveness made me realize that it was time to throw out a bluff. "Sure, I got the box, but until I get B.J., nobody gets nothing."

His familiar looking eyes seem to light up. "Adams, check back around 11:00 tonight. I might be able to make a deal for you."

"Sure, I'll be here."

Fall From Apocalypse

So now I had an ace up my sleeve. I couldn't locate the eastside boys or Frailey's son, but I had a meet set-up. I was close to getting B.J. Yet, their was something that bothered me about Bumpy Morgan. I couldn't put my finger on it. Why was the operator of a dive in the Bowery so connected that he could set up a meeting this important. I was missing something.

I left Bumpy's and strolled up town, out of the misery and despair to the sunshine of possibilities for the few. I ran into my new friend, Wayne Frye, at Hunter College of CUNY on Park Avenue. He was a southern boy who was recently hired as a professor there, and we had met when B.J. took a class from him in marketing. For some reason, she felt that she needed to figure out a way to more effectively market my business. She and Frye hit it off, and we shared some interesting times with him. When he asked about her, I just said she was busy on a case, engaged in some small talk and excused myself. He was only 24 years old, and thought, as the youngest professor at CUNY, that he was some sort of whiz-kid marketing guru. He was an O.K. guy, but he had a lot to learn about the real world. Like many academics, he had some solid book-learning, but he had no worthwhile experience with the real world the average Joe had to live in. Well, he was in New York, now. He would learn alright, and if he survived, he would learn that the real world was a lot different than the cloistered walls of academia.

Fall From Apocalypse

I cut over to Broadway and 8th Avenue. I headed over to Bill Shore's place. It was almost 7:00 o'clock and time for a sandwich. The place was packed, but Bill found me a place at the end of the bar. After the guy who was sitting next to me fell off the stool several times, I helped him to the door and into a cab. I went back to sit down and a couple of blonds had decided to flop down on the stools. I headed back out the door and grinned at Bill on the way out.

Darkness was approaching. Darkness – I had always loved it. Even in Korea, during the war, I had prayed for darkness, back when I believed there was someone to listen to prayers. Knowing the enemy would be coming over the ridges in their tennis shoes once darkness approached, I anticipated it with glee back when I actually believed I was fighting for something worthwhile. What a chump! I would squeeze the trigger of the machine gun and watch the sky light up with the tracers as the gun played that sweet rat-a-tat-tat symphony. Ah, the sounds were magnified in the darkness, as I thought that each bullet that seared the flesh of those dirty little commies was the goddamn sweet sound of American righteousness bringing the enemies of freedom to their knees. Yeah, what a chump. I was defending a system that used me and every other member of the non-privileged class to serve at the altar of those who manipulated and controlled the populace with bull-shit democracy propaganda.

J. Wayne Frye

Fall From Apocalypse

A car pulled alongside me and a familiar voice said, "get in."

I nearly went for the 45, but I caught myself in time. John Havoc had the back door of the police cruiser open. I was still lost in my thoughts of another time and another war, as I almost trance-like crawled into the back seat beside Havoc.

I noticed his front teeth had some black residue on them. I figured he must have had some chocolate cake and forgot to lick his teeth.

He said, "any leads?"

Somewhat surprised, I replied, "leads for what?"

"B.J."

"How'd you know?"

"I pick up things fast Aaron. Faster than you sometimes. I've got my connections."

"The organization has her, and I am going to get her. It is that simple, man."

He eased toward me. "No it isn't that simple. You see, the big boys have come in on this. Washington is interested."

I cut in sharply. "The FBI?"

"They sent a man up special. My guess is that he is just one of many Washington boys who are interested. CIA, NSA, maybe even the Secret Service. This thing is big, Aaron. Really big."

"They riding herd?"

He took a deep breath as the car rounded a corner and headed up Central Park East. "Aaron, they want you out. Not just out of the case, but out of town. They seem to think you are fouling the whole works up."

"Out! Goddamn those Washington bureaucrats! I'm in, baby!" I leaned in close to John, as the driver peered back over his shoulder in response to my outburst. "You tell them that I'm goddamn in – in to stay." I made a symbol with my thumb and index finger. "I'm that close. And those bastards start sticking their noses in, and they'll gum up the whole works. I'm close, too goddamn close."

John eased back and said, "I figured you were. So, you have that box the Washington boys and the organization are looking for?"

"Maybe."

"OK, Aaron. You know how I feel about B.J. I will keep the Washington boys off your back, but 24 hours may be stretching it. So, whatever you have to do, get it done soon."

Fall From Apocalypse

"Well, I got something positive in the works for tonight, but I'd like to located Howard Frailey's son as back-up in case what I have on-the-line doesn't pan out. Any ideas where I might find him?"

"OK, now we get down to brass tacks. What you know about Howard Frailey?"

"I don't know the man. All I asked about was his son."

A look of disgust crept across John's face. "You know him aright. Seems like someone with a lawn mowing fetish sliced him into bite size pieces. You know who might have done it?"

"A conscientious citizen, probably. Someone who wanted to clean up the city a little. Too bad they don't have any grass down on Wall Street or around the banks. Those boys could use a little trimming, too."

"You'll get yours one day, Aaron."

"What about Frailey's son?"

"Heard of the Bluebeards? They have a place on Euclid. They are at war right now with the Eastside Easies. Frailey is an Easy. Been two kills the last week. We are hoping they'll all kill each other. Check with the Bluebeards. They'll know."

"Thanks, John. You going to keep the Feds off my back?"

"I'll try. But 24 hours is about it." He patted the driver on the shoulder and told him to go to Euclid.

John pointed out the boarded up building used as a meeting place by the Bluebeards, shook my hand, slammed the door and sped away.

Euclid was the type of place reserved for those who were on the margins of a society based on greed. Only the less fortunate of society had to live there among the miscreants who survived by preying on others. This was a direct result of a society that did not care for the less fortunate. These were the throw-a-ways of a nation that had no compassion.

It was nearly 9:00 o'clock and the whole street appeared completely deserted, but I knew it wasn't. I had picked that up the minute I stepped into John's car. We had been followed since I left Bill Shore's place, and the car stopped about a hundred feet from where John let me off. One man had gotten out. He was waiting for me, waiting somewhere in the darkness, thinking he could use the cover of night to nail me. Little did he know that the that darkness was my light. I was home in the darkness. I embraced it, caressed it, wrapped myself in it and felt safe.

Fall From Apocalypse

Ignoring the guy who had disappeared into the darkness down the street, I noticed a light on in the old building, but as I slid one of the doors aside to step in, it was quickly extinguished. I cut the darkness like thunder. "Any son-of-a-bitch who moves gets it. In fact, some who don't move will get it. I can't see a goddamn thing, but the first sound I hear activates this 45 I have in my hand. Now, somebody move real easy toward the light. Move! I want to see you sons-a-bitches."

Some guy with a shiny buckle moved toward the light and switched it on. It was about a forty watt bulb, but bright enough for the four young punks to see that I had a death dealer in my hand.

"O.K., who is the big cheese here?" I leaned back against the wall beside the makeshift door, so I could pivot toward the doorway if my friend outside decided to intrude.

A tall, fat, slimy bastard with a grin like Richard Widmark in the movie where he pushed the old lady in a wheelchair down the stairs, stepped toward me.

Tilting my head slightly and wiggling my gun a bit, I said, "don't come too close man."

I looked down at my forty-five and continued. "My friend here might be offended by your body odour. That is far enough."

"Sure man, sure. I know you. Fellows this here is a real live private eye. A real tough 'un, too. Name's Adams, Aaron Adams. I seen your picture plenty a times." He smiled at me, gesturing with his right hand and continued. "I'm Clancy, leader of this here bunch. That over there is Bob Hilton," he said pointing to a goon with a hypodermic needle in his hands, "and that's Gore Martin," again he pointed toward his comrade. This one was just as ugly as Hilton, and he had a rubber ball in his left hand that he kept squeezing.

Clancy grinned, showing his rotten teeth, but who could blame him. The people in the ghetto couldn't afford to go to the dentist. Still grinning, he pointed to the last guy, who looked like a pygmy. "Geeley Mason. He's our secret weapon. Real expert with a tire tool."

"Yeah, you all look real tough."

They looked at each other and began to laugh as Clancy said, "hey man, you goddamn right. We are the toughest. Put your gun away. We ain't got no beef against you."

I eased the 45 back into the holster and sat down on a stack of cinder blocks to my left, leaving the coat open in case I needed to pull the rod quickly. "So, you boys having a rumble tonight?"

Clancy replied, "yeah, you interested?"

Fall From Apocalypse

"Sure, I always like to see a good show."

"Sorry, this is a private affair tonight. Maybe another time." After uttering that, Clancy jumped up on the table like some kind of jack rabbit.

Meanwhile the guy with the hypodermic sprawled out on the floor and looked up at me and shouted, "yeah, ain't nobody gonna be in Shepherd's Alley tonight but us and them. We gonna…"

Before he could finish, Clancy was off the table and put his boots on Hilton's left thigh. I eased back a bit more and watched him play leader. "Shut your goddamn mouth. You stupid bastard." Then Clancy turned toward me. "Private, Adams, private. This here is a private affair, real private. Only four of our gang and four of them. Understand?"

"Sure, Clancy."

I eased toward the door. "Maybe next time."

He looked confused at my complacency and said, "yeah, maybe we'll bring you and your friend there in your pocket into one of our more classy rumbles."

I turned my back on the hoods and stepped through the boards back onto the sidewalk. I immediately surveyed the street up and down, straight ahead, then turned to check the roof behind me. The guy was a pro, a real pro. He knew how to stay hidden. Only one way to make him come out of the dark, expose myself.

I leaned under what was left of an awning, pulled the forty-five and made a dash across the street, nearly falling on the curb. Half way across, I heard something move at the far end of the street. I did not bother to check it out, since I was in mid-street. That was for amateurs. When you're exposed, you don't look for the enemy. You move and you move damn fast to a predetermined spot. My spot was a cluster of trash cans up against some steps. I dived over them, feeling the lining of my coat rip as I banged against the wall. Spinning around in a crouch, I expected bullets to be whizzing all around me, but, to my surprise, there was only silence. Silence except for the sound of my own heavy breathing. I looked toward the Bluebeard's hideout and saw the light had been turned out. They had probably left by a back way and were headed to Shepherd's Alley and the rumble. I had to get there right away. If I didn't get there first, Frailey's son might slip through my fingers. I had to chance it.

I took off my trench coat and placed it in a trash can. This guy was a pro, and a light coloured coat would make it too easy for him. I turned up the collar on my suit jacket, buttoned it up to conceal as much of it as possible. Then I crawled as far as I could behind the trash cans without exposing myself.

I looked down the street about a hundred feet at an old abandoned car propped up on blocks. If I could get there, I could make it around the corner and maybe safety. I didn't hesitate. Up and running, running like a son-of-a-bitch. I felt the cool air hitting my face, as I saw the abandoned car draw nearer and nearer. Then I saw it! There was only one light on the street, a lamp post hanging over the abandoned car. The glare of the light in the windshield showed me death. It was in the form of a man who had stepped onto the street and was taking careful aim with a gun. A pro? Hell, he was the number one pro of all time. How many killers took the time to be sure? The bastard was skilled, all skilled. In the windshield, I saw that he had the gun extended in his left hand and was using his right arm as a brace to steady the trigger hand. A left-handed killer. I had only seen one before. It had been years ago in Cairo. He was a cold, calculating Arab who hired out all over the world at top dollar. I had shot him in the back, because he was the kind of guy you didn't face. Well, he was dead, but this guy was very much alive. The son-of-a-bitch had me. Had me in his grasp. How he must have enjoyed the pure ecstasy of seeing me run, but knowing all the time he had me. But why didn't he fire. Even if he missed, I was still too far from the car to make it.

Fall From Apocalypse

It was too late for me to do anything but stop, crumble to the ground and try to at least take him with a fireback as I died. He had me. There was no way out. Suddenly a drop of sweat burned my eyes and I blinked. Damn, was I dreaming? One blink of the eye, and I expected to look at his reflection in the windshield, as he squeezed off a round to end my life. But, what did I see? Nothing. He just disappeared.

I crawled the few feet to the car and rolled under the right fender. The forty-five was out and aimed where he had been, but the street was empty. A goddamn pro alright. Hell, I wasn't dreaming. The bastard saw his own reflection, knew I might stand a chance and backed off. Hell, yes! This guy was dynamite. Too good for most, but I had him rattled. He knew me or knew about me, and he was scared. He wasn't gambling. The kill was out, and the organization had hired a top man. Maybe the top man.

Looking up the street, I caught a glimpse of what had to be the toe of a shoe. It was sticking out from behind a stairway leading to the entrance of a boarded up building. Yeah, he was smart, but not too smart. I let out a satisfied grin, eased slightly to the right of the concrete block, took careful aim and squeezed the trigger. The sound of the gun cut through the silence like a bomb blast. I scored a direct hit, but all I hit was an empty shoe. It slithered three or four feet on the sidewalk, and I knew what it was like to be up against a real pro. This guy was sharp.

I dived back completely under the car just as a bullet tore into the pavement, missing my head by only a hair. I thought that it was a good thing he was using a silencer, because that cut down on accuracy, but some killers are lost without them. They needed them for security. The Arab from Cairo had used one, too. Yet, I was sure this guy didn't use it for that reason. He was cold and calculating. He was playing with me, teasing me just enough to let me know he could call the shots. He had me again. I was trapped under the car, afraid to make a move, because I didn't know where he was. Hell, the son-of-a-bitch could be up in the driver's seat for all I knew.

I rolled on my back and tried to figure a way out. I glanced down between my legs and saw the headlights of a car come on. It started up and cruised my way. I pulled back the hammer on the forty-five and waited. The car didn't slow down. It just breezed right by, but a small cylinder, the type used for expensive cigars was tossed from a window and rolled under the car.

I rolled on my stomach, saw the car pull up to the far curb and the pro got in. He was still playing it smart. He made sure I didn't have time for a shot. The back door was opened by the driver, and he dived in head first.

Fall From Apocalypse

I caught a glimpse of his feet, one with a shoe on and the other with nothing but a white sock. Not very stylish I though. The Arab had worn white socks. The car lurched forward and sped around the corner. I was safe, but why? Why go to all the trouble of setting me up and then cutting out when the job was a certainty?

I crawled out, brushed my clothes off and looked at my watch, 9:30. I had to get to Shepherd's Alley. I almost forgot the cigar container, but I had pulled it out with me. I reached down, picked it up, looked inside and pulled out a small piece of paper that said: *We have Holden. You have 48 hours to deliver the box. If we don't get it by 9:00 AM Friday morning, then we start to work on Holden. You have no choice. Believe us, we have the man who can take you. You should know that by now.*

The box, the goddamn box. What was so important about the box. And then there was B.J. She knew something about it, too. Forty-eight hours! Well, I still had time. Maybe Frailey's son was the key to locating B.J. I'd give it a try. I didn't have the box, so I had to come up with something in forty-eight hours. The box I could not locate, but maybe I could located B.J.

I waited in Shepherd's Alley. There was something in the air – that certain twinge of excitement. Something was about to unfold.

Fall From Apocalypse

I waited in between the buildings that led to Shepherd's Alley for nearly 20 minutes at a time when every second was precious, but what else could I do? The clock was ticking on the forty-eight hours, and I did not have the box.

Just as I was about to give up and leave, there was that old feeling. The feeling you get just before you are about to go into battle. There was something wicked headed my way. I could feel that anticipation, that pounding of the heart as one prepares for confrontation, knowing that death awaits either you or the enemy.

The time was ripe for a rumble. Suddenly, the Bluebeards appeared at the far end of the alley like a whiff of smoke conjured up by a magician. Clancy was breathing heavily, his chest rising up and down rhythmically. Martin's eyes were glazed with that opium stare. Hilton was grinning like a kid who had seen his first titty. They were all primed and ready - ready for that one moment of glory, that moment of ecstasy when the blade of a knife slides into some poor bastard's flesh. Yeah, there was pleasure in death and pain. Why not? All these hoods were products of a society based on violence. They saw no way out of the predicament that society dictated for them. They were the rubbish of a nation that discarded those deemed unfit for hope and opportunity. They were the victims of a society that defined everyone by the size of their bank account rather than the content of their character – a society where your pedigree, rather than your ability was a ticket to a good job and a life of material abundance.

These guys were victims, but I did not have time to contemplate the reasons they lived the life they did. All that mattered was locating B.J. and saving her from being the victim of those who saw most of humanity as a commodity to be bartered and used, then discarded. The government, the corporations and the organization were all the same. Lives were bought and sold one way or another. You could die in useless foreign wars defending the so-called democracy that Americans were propagandized into believing they had, in the domestic corporate wars of worker domination so the rich could get richer or in some stupid war over turf in the ghettos of despair promulgated as a result of a corrupt society that refused a hand up for those in need. There was no difference. I had learned that the hard way.

What was about to occur in Shepherd's Alley I had seen many times in many places in one form or another. I had killed, and I must admit that in many instances there was great satisfaction in dispatching a bastard before he dispatched me. Life and death was power. It was Mao who said "power comes from the barrel of a gun." He was so right. The USA proved that time and time again when it used its weapons of destruction to make other nations cower in fear.

Fall From Apocalypse

Yet, I was only a spectator. I did not care who lived and died in that alley. They were all forced to be scavengers by a society that created the conditions that bred those who saw no hope. All I wanted was Frailey. Just one word with him!

The Eastside Boys came into the alley from the opposite side, the moonlight casting an eerie glow on their lavender jackets. Standing with an erect and bold countenance, one sensed they were mighty gods from the land of death – four gods come to do battle with their kind. And when the spectre of battle was over, the survivors would return to their lair to lick their wounds and prepare for another battle to affirm their worth in a nation where violence was the only hope for those suffering the disdain and contempt of the rich and powerful. Unfortunately, they practiced their violence on their fellow sojourners in the land of despair, rather than marching on the enclaves of the rich to destroy those who kept them in bondage. I knew what the problem was, but I was only one man. I could not change the world by myself, and the poor and middle class people who lined up for their invisible chains were too wrapped up in religion and patriotic babble to see where the real problems lay in a society based on greed. Hell, I did not have time to be philosophical. I was prepared to kill these miscreant, discarded vultures if necessary, because the only thing that mattered to me in life was my beloved B.J.

Fall From Apocalypse

I stepped out of the darkness, where I could be seen and bellowed, "hold your rumble, boys. First, I get my pleasure."

Clancy, wrenching his knife in his hand, shouted, "Adam's, you ain't got no business here. None, you hear me!"

I reached inside my coat pocket and came out with the great equalizer, the death dealer, the god of fire-power. The 4forty-five looked like a cannon when I stepped back, leaned against the building wall and levelled it first at Clancy, then the leader of the Eastside Boys.

Smiling, raising and lowering my gun, I said, "my friend here says I got business in this alley. And if I don't like what I hear about my business, my friend will do some talking."

Clancy, puffing out his chest decided to act tough. "We can take you man. We can take you. There's eight of us and you only got six shoots with that cannon."

"Well, you are almost right Clancy. If you knew your Colt 45's, you'd know that I use the old model. The one that holds seven rounds. So, that means I'd only be able to kill seven of you. Who do you think I am going to shot first though, Clancy? Take a wild guess who is guaranteed not to be the last man standing."

Fall From Apocalypse

When I said that, he froze in his tracks and gave my remarks some serious thought and finally said, "OK, OK, what is your pleasure man?"

"I have no interest in you Clancy, unless you just want to die. Then, I can certainly accommodate you. I want Frailey from the Eastside Boys."

As I said that, the leader of the Eastside Boys stepped forward and decided to play his role as head honcho by sounding tough. "Hey man, suppose he ain't with us? That is a possibility you know."

I frowned broadly. "He's with you, and if I don't get him, I'll gun everyone of you bastards down just for the fun of it. I don't need blood. Don't misunderstand me, I love blood – love watching it pour out of the holes I make in bastards like you, but it is your call. I can talk to Frailey, or my friend here can talk to everyone of you, and believe me, my friend here has a real vulgar way of talking."

Knowing that I wasn't playing games, he turned to a skinny kid who looked like he was a geek from those old freak shows that used to be a part of every carnival. Half his nose was gone from a tangle with a knife, and from what was left of his face, it looked like the knife had had an incredibly good time. He told Frailey, "talk to the man."

Fall From Apocalypse

Frailey walked a few feet toward me and I said, "far enough, asshole."

He stopped and said, "what you want, man?"

"Frailey, your old man is dead. I mowed the bastard up. I know you were in on B.J.'s kidnapping. Don't deny it. Don't even shake your head. I want just one thing from you, and if you don't give it to me, I'm going to blow your goddamn brains out, after I shoot you in the balls first. You dig me, boy?"

His face was as red as a baby's bottom with diaper rash. "You son-of-bitch. You mother….."

I cut in before he finished. "I didn't come here to listen to name calling. I have a question and I better get the answer I want."

He came at me like a madman. Before he had covered half the distance, the other three were right behind him. I pivoted slightly to my left and straight armed him with my left hand. His head hit the wall, and I gave him an elbow in the ribs. The other three bastards kept coming. The one in the middle got the first shot in the stomach and he crumbled to the pavement, desperately trying to hold his guts in. I dropped to my knees and kept pulling the trigger. One of the others caught it in the neck and fell to my left. The last bastard dived for me, but was he met in mid-air with 12 cents of

J. Wayne Frye

hot lead.

I scrambled to my feet, never taking my eyes off Clancy, suspecting that he might decide to side with his enemies in going after me. "Keep loose, Clancy. Keep it loose. I lost count of how many bullets I have left, but I think it is four. That is just enough,"

"We're cool, daddy! Real cool." He was scared shitless.

Meantime, Frailey had managed to get to his feet and was leaning against the wall, bending over in pain from the jab I gave him in the ribs. He was even more scared than Clancy.

"B.J., man, B.J."

"Man, please. Please! I don't know!"

I looked down at his right hand that was twitching by his side, pulled the trigger and blew his thumb off. I grinned as he fell to the ground, whimpering like a baby. I reached into my coast pocket, pulled out some ammo and reloaded the gun. I spun the barrel for maximum scare effect and levelled it at his head.

He was really shaking now, as he realized I was not a man to be trifled with. He pleaded with me. "God man, this is big. Too big for you and me."

Fall From Apocalypse

I leaned in a little closer. "Nothing is too big for this forty-five Frailey, including you and the whole damn organization. I love pulling the trigger. You want to suffer some more?"

"Please, please! They will kill me. My dad wasn't suppose to tell me anything. They just used me for the snatch. I ain't nobody, never have been, never will be. I was just a scumbag to my dad and the whole damn organization. But I'm telling you. They will kill me!"

"Take your pick, Frailey. Chance getting out of town to escape the organization, or face my wrath. Believe me, you don't want to even think about my wrath. I make the organization boys look like school children. I've been trained by the best killing organization in the world, the U.S. government. I am going to ask only one more time, and then I start the torture. I hope you don't answer, because I haven't tortured anybody in several hours, I am getting real antsy."

Sobbing almost uncontrollably, he muttered "Saint Dominique. That is it. It is some island in the Caribbean near Haiti. The organization bought the whole island from Papa Doc Duvalier, and turned it into a haven for drugs, gambling and any other vice you want to practice. They had her flown down there to keep the heat off. They's too many people trying to locate her and get to that goddamn box everyone wants."

Fall From Apocalypse

I cocked the hammer back. He began to vomit. "Please, please, Adams! I had to help with the snatch. I had to do it. My old man made me!"

I grabbed what was left of his right hand and shot the other four fingers off one at a time. I decided to let him live, but as I turned to leave, I said, "I had to Frailey. I just had to blow your fingers off!"

I thought to myself that is the problem with the world. Nobody, but nobody will stand up to authority. Almost everyone was like Frailey, too intimidated to take a stand. I looked over at Clancy and stared a hole through him. He knew what I was capable of. He signalled his comrades, and they beat it as a siren began to wail in the distance.

I walked out of the alley to the sounds of the still whimpering Frailey into the well-lit street. Out of the darkness into the light. It was almost as if the sun were shining. But, on a small island off the coast of Haiti, B.J. was waiting. When I got there the sun wouldn't shine, because Aaron Adams would blot it out with the blaze of a gun. Tomorrow, maybe I would be lucky. Tomorrow would be the day of the gun.

CHAPTER 9
THE LONG SWIM BACK INTO BJ's ARMS

NOTE TO YOUNG READERS

Keep in mind while reading this chapter, that this story takes place in 1969. This was a time before mass paranoia took hold across the world when it comes to security. There were no metal detectors, no x-ray machines, no body scans and no pat-downs. People actually walked aboard planes without fear that a terrorist might be among the passengers. In fact, carrying a weapon on a plane in the USA would not lead to an airport shutdown or an assumption that you were a terrorist. It was a much different world, for better or worse, than the one in which we live today.

On the way to the airport, I called John from a phone booth on 6th and Broadway and advised him on the latest link to B.J. He wanted to come with me, but I convinced him to stay in the city, and see if he could fend off the feds for 48 hours. I also told him to contact Bumpy Morgan to tell him I would be in touch with him in a couple of days in regards to the box, if I did not rescue B.J.

That was when he said, "Aaron, you do have the box don't you? You aren't putting these guys on are you? You can deliver it? That box is really important. It has to be protected."

Fall From Apocalypse

Lying, I said, "sure, I got it."

I was a little disappointed in John. He seemed more worried about the box than B.J.

I finished our conversation by asking how Freddie was doing. John, sort of laughing said, "he told me to tell you to save the guy with the sawed-off shotgun for him."

That was Freddy. He'd be alright, because he was like me. He wouldn't let them throw any dirt over him until he got even.

The only flight direct to Saint Dominique was Central Caribbean Charter Airlines. I was told there was no space available, but American Airlines had a flight at 9:00AM. It was 11:30 PM. I could not afford to wait. I was seriously thinking about pulling my forty-five, kidnapping the pilot and hijacking the plane when I asked if there were any private charters available. The guy said that there was a pilot named Dink in the south terminal who flew a Lear Jet that would have to refuel in Miami, but if I was willing to pay the high price, he would probably take me, if he wasn't booked by his usual employer, the Strand Corporation. He knew Dink was there, because he had just received a call from him less than five minutes ago.

Getting directions, I was off to the south terminal. How interesting I thought, I knew all about the Strand Corporation. It was an organization front.

It had been run by the mob for years after they took it over, when labour unrest nearly bankrupted it, and the owners had been forced to sell out to the mob. Hell, it was the mob that had fomented the labour unrest to start with. Then, when they took it over, they strong-armed the unions and got even more concessions than the original owners had asked for. Just another nail in the working man's coffin. From union bosses to CEO's, it didn't matter. The only ones who came out on top were the rich and powerful, while the rest of society begged for a crumbs. It would be interesting to meet Dink. No doubt, he was more than just a pilot. Yet, I had no choice. B.J.'s life hung in the balance.

The terminal was reached through a long, meandering corridor, then an open area that led to what looked like a leftover World War II Quonset hut. The metal door was open, so I walked in. The cavernous building was deserted, except for a muscular man of about 40 with a pock-marked face, who was sitting at an old desk talking on the phone. He looked up at me like I was obviously lost, as he said, "wait up for me baby, I'll be finished here in about five minutes."

It was appropriate for Dink to be in the south terminal. He spoke with a deep southern accent.

Fall From Apocalypse

This dude had obviously made it into the organization based on something other than his ethnicity.

He slammed the phone down like he didn't appreciate me popping in that late on him, as I said, "you're name Dink?"

He gave me a look of disdain and said, "that's me, bud. Sorry, you must be in the wrong place. This is a private terminal for the Strand Corporation. Only company employees are allowed in here, and I don't know you."

"You the pilot?"

"That's me."

"I need to go to Saint Dominique. I got some big bucks if you will fly me down."

"Hey, the big boys let me pick up a few dollars extra on occasion by flying private charters, but I would have to know what business you have in Saint Dominique first and get their OK. You going down for a few days of high-rolling?"

"No, I'm going down on some personal business."

"OK, it will cost you $250 an hour for fuel, $150 an hour for the plane and $100 an hour for me. I can probably take you in a few days, as long as the big boys uptown approve it."

Determined, I replied. "Need to go there right now!"

He let out a laugh and got up. "No way, Jose. Impossible."

That was when I decided that I did not have time to negotiate. I pulled out the forty-five and levelled it at his mid-section. He had seen plenty of guns before, probably had plenty pulled on him, as it showed in his demeanour. He was not afraid, just cautious.

"You're making a big mistake mister. You don't know who you're dealing with here, and I'm not just talking about me."

"I know who I am dealing with Dink. I'm not afraid of the organization. I've dispatched plenty of you hoods over the years. I enjoy it."

Now, he was getting a little worried. The quizzical look on his face did not necessitate him asking me who I was. I just let it out. "Name's Adams, Aaron Adams."

That was all it took. Now, he was scared. "Listen Adams, I don't give a damn about your beef with the organization. I know your rep, and you don't need to impress me. Just tell me what you want, and I will try to accommodate you."

"First, I want you to reach into your breast coat pocket and remove your heater very carefully. Then toss it to the back of the room."

Dink complied by tossing his gun against the far wall and said, "you're crazy man. Anyway, the Lear doesn't carry enough fuel to make it all the way. We'll have to stop in Miami to refuel. When the big boys hear about this, they'll have every landing field, no matter how small, between here and Key West covered."

"Then we won't stop in Miami."

"You some kind of lunatic? The plane can only fly six hours without refuelling. Saint Dominique is seven hours, provided you don't have to buck a head wind."

I gave him the death smile. "Then you better pray for a heavy tail wind to increase your speed. If we run out of fuel, you can ditch it, and we'll swim the rest of the way."

"Adams, the word has been put out on you. You'll never make it. You go to Saint Dominique and you're a dead man. Half of the organization is down there this time of the year. Man, it is suicide."

"Suicide is what you're committing by running you mouth. Let's go."

"OK, OK, you won't get an argument out of me. I am just a pilot. That's all I am, just a goddamn pilot."

He shrugged his shoulders, turned and headed out the door toward the plane. It took us about 10 minutes before we were cleared for takeoff. Dink was drenched with sweat caused due to his intense fear by the time we were over Baltimore control. That was when I said, "relax, Dink." I don't always kill you organization boys. You do a good job, and I may let you live."

"Adams, I'm a good pilot, but not good enough to fly on vapours. You have no control over whether I live or die, because we are both going into the drink. That's a fact, if you don't let me refuel."

"You better get this flying hearse up high enough then to glide into Saint Dominique. No stops."

After we passed Key West control there was no turning back. Gas or no gas, we were committed. Dink was scared. Hell, maybe I was, too, but without B.J., I had nothing to live for anyway.

I licked my lips and said, "how much further?"

Fall From Apocalypse

"About an hour, but we're on empty. You're committing suicide. Goddamn it Adams, you're a stupid son-of-a-bitch."

"Actually, you're the stupid one, Dink. You see, if you didn't work for the organization, you wouldn't even be here, now. You picked the wrong line of work."

He reached up to nervously wipe away the sweat from his brow and started to breath heavily. "Damn it! We're out of gas. You're getting us both killed."

"I still hear the whirr of the engine. So relax Dink. Why not cut your engine and glide for awhile?"

"Great idea, Adams. Only trouble is what if there isn't enough gas to restart the engine? Then, we are in the drink."

I gave him the cold, calculating look. "I'll breathe fire into the engine, because I'm hotter than a stick of TNT."

He took a deep breath and shut-off the engines. The silence was deafening. The only sound was the wind rushing by outside, as we floated like a leaf falling from the top of a tree.

"How much further, Dink?"

Fall From Apocalypse

"I'd say 30 to 45 minutes. We are 25,000 feet, so maybe 30, if we are lucky. 30 minutes we might make it, but 45, no way."

"Then, I guess we better hope for 30."

When the altitude hit 20,000 feet, he restarted the engines and ran them for about 5 minutes. Then he cut them off and glided for about 10 minutes until he hit 10,000 feet. He restarted them. They caught, but then immediately cut off.

Shaking his head with disgust, he said, "we've bought it. Goddamn you! You are absolutely insane."

I looked at the horizon and the sky was a deep purple as the morning sun began to appear, glimmering on the sea that heaved slowly with the dancing, unruffled, grand, majestic waves bathed with crimson light. Life was that sunrise, the life of B.J. I saw it. There it was in the far distance, the island.

There is a silent thread in the mind that burns with the profitable flames of hope. Fixing my eyes on the land in the distance, it was like a beacon fire glowing brightly with the spirit and strength of the love I felt for B.J.

Desperately struggling with the wheel as he pulled back on it, trying to stay airborne, Dink said, "we're going into the sea, asshole. We can't make it!"

"Keep your hands on the wheel. We can make it."

"You're too optimistic. There's no way! We'll be lucky if those huge waves don't break the plane apart.

We continued to glide about 15 minutes until the altitude hit 1500 feet. He was becoming frantic. "Adams, this is it. We've got maybe another 5 minutes, and we are still at least 25 or 30 kilometres from shore. We are on the back side of the island, which is uninhabited. Nobody is going to see us go down. You have to let me contact Haiti Control so someone will know where we are. They will send out rescue aircraft for us; otherwise, we have no chance."

"Yeah, and then the big boys get word I am here, looking for B.J. Shut up, and sit this bird down as well as you can. You have any life jackets on board?"

"Yeah, back in the cabin. They are in the locker."

Feeling some camaraderie with Dink due to our circumstances, I was no longer worried about keeping my 45 cocked and ready. I shouldered it and said, "anything we could rip out and use for a raft?"

"A raft? Hell Adams, what makes you think the plane is not going to break apart the second we hit the water?"

Smiling, I said, "well, you don't have to put it down in one piece. But if you don't, I'm following you to hell and kicking your sorry ass all over the goddamn place."

For some reason, at that moment in time, he liked me, I could see it on his face. He let out a half grin and told me to rip out the bar top in the back cabin to use as a raft. Circumstances can often make allies out of enemies. The predicament we were in made us comrades in a fight for survival.

Just as I finished ripping out the top of the bar, Dink called for me to come up front. Pointing at my seat, he said, "buckle up and brace your legs against the instrument panel, but before you do it, look straight ahead."

We were almost there, maybe within 10 kilometres. "Can we make it to land?"

"No way, we're going into the water."

"We're close enough, I can swim that far."

Fall From Apocalypse

"You know Adams, I hope I live long enough to see them get you first. I'd like to see just how much guts you really got."

Confused, I said, "they?

"Yeah, they! This is the south side of the uninhabited part of the island. It is deserted except for a few wild beasts and the water isn't fit for swimming. That's why it was never developed. It's not that the beaches aren't any good, but people don't swim here, because it is a feeding ground for tiger sharks," he said as he curled his lips into a half smile, hoping to see me crumble when I came face-to-face with death.

"I rubbed my brow with my left hand and spoke softly, "I'll bet they aren't afraid of a 45 either, are they?"

He let out a half laugh. "They aren't afraid of a battleship."

Looking out at the ocean that seemed to be getting closer and closer, Dink said, "get ready. Brace yourself. The surf is pretty high. We could start cart wheeling."

I have to give the guy credit. He sat it down like he was landing at Kennedy. Just a few bumps and then silence except for the waves slapping up against the fuselage.

I was pretty impressed with his ability and said, "nice job, Dink."

"Yeah, nice job landing us in a shark den. Grab your life jacket and lets get out of her. Unfortunately, I don't have any shark repellent on board."

I grabbed the bar top on the way to the back door, and stood there with my life jacket on while Dink reached behind a counter and pulled out two ice picks. I dropped the bar top and started to reach for my forty-five, and he said, "Christ man, we need these to make sure the sharks that come after us will at least know we didn't go easy."

I liked the guy. He had guts. I grabbed the counter top and tossed it into the water. The salty ocean breeze felt refreshing as the morning air slapped us in the face. We dived into the water side-by-side, grabbed the counter top and started paddling toward shore. I turned to him and said, "how long will it take us to get there you figure?"

"Maybe an hour, maybe two. But only the part of us that is left will make it." With his last word, he pointed about 300 feet straight ahead. It was one big son-of-a-bitch. Maybe twenty feet long and was headed straight for us. Sharks were no different than most of the people in the world of commerce. They see someone at a disadvantage and they pounce on them.

Fall From Apocalypse

"You can try shooting it," he said as he handed me one of the ice picks, "but when you run out of bullets, this might come in handy."

I decided to save my bullets, so I transferred the pick from my left to my right hand. I started removing my life jacket. Damned if I was going to be cramped up in it while battling a shark. I heaved the jacket in the direction of the shark, and the bastard just gobbled it up without stopping. This wasn't just a shark. It was a beast from the very bowels of hell itself. It seemed to pick up speed and move straight toward us, I turned to Dink and shook my head in disbelief. "Dink, that bastard looks like a torpedo."

"I don't understand it! It shouldn't be attacking us like this. They generally circle about first. We don't stand a chance."

"Hell, we're breathing aren't we? And as long as we are, we've got a chance. We blind the bastard first. Go for the eyes."

Twenty feet away, the shark opened its jaws and I could smell its putrid breath. It was trying to devour everything in sight, the bar top and us both.

That was its mistake. I leaped off to the right and jabbed the ice pick into its left eye. I nearly lost the pick, but managed to pull it out just as its side brushed against me. Dink had already given up and was frantically swimming toward the distant shore.

I bobbed up and down in the water and got ready for the shark's next charge. As blood filled the water from the stabbed eye, the beast was now more enraged than ever. Its remaining eye was determinedly fixated on me, and you could see hatred in it. The monster of the sea was going to make me pay.

I reached for my 45, aimed at the eye and just started pulling the trigger. Three shots and I had obliterated the eye. The bastard was totally blind, but that did not stop him. He just kept coming, sensing where I was. His jaws were wide open. I pivoted to the right, grabbed onto its fin just as I pocketed the 45. It started to dive.

With the ice pick still in my hand, I was stabbing away furiously. Finally, I fell off when we were about 50 feet below the surface. Struggling upwards, my eyes were burning intensely from the salt water and just as I was about to give up and ingest water, I hit the surface, desperately gasping for air.

Looking around me, I located the creature and prepare for the next charge, but quickly realized there would not to be one. Dink's screaming told me why.

Fall From Apocalypse

He was bobbing up and down, swaying from side to side like a buoy, his left arm ripped off at the elbow. I shouted, "hold on man, hold on," as I swam toward him. My arms flailing wildly, desperately trying to reach him, the bitter taste of salt water began to fill my lungs and I started to cough and wheeze.

He did not reply. The terror stamped on his face and the sudden jerking movement told me what was happening. The shark was ripping his legs off beneath the surface. I continued to frantically swim toward Dink, all the time knowing it was a hopeless endeavour. All I could do was use the shark's occupation with him to my advantage. I leaped toward the shark and started stabbing madly into its side. As the ocean turned red all about me, I finally dropped the ice pick from sheer exhaustion as my hand cramped up.

Dink's torso bobbed to the surface in a cockeyed fashion due to the lack of symmetry in his mangled body. His right leg was shirred off at the knee and his left leg and hip were gone.

I assumed I had finally killed the shark, but as I reached out toward Dink, the shark roared to the surface with Dink's leg stuck between its giant teeth. Amazingly, Dink was still alive as he looked at me with pleading eyes. His look of desperation was obliterated in the blinking of an eye, as the shark clamped down on his head, taking it off at the neck. All that was left was his chest, still wrapped in a life jacket, floating precariously in the water.

This minion of evil from the depths of hell still had an insatiable blood lust that was not satisfied. Somehow, he sensed where I was and headed in my direction. Then, I saw the ice pick floating on the surface. Reaching out, I managed to grip it in my still cramping hand. My body was wracked with pain, but the thought of B.J. gave me a surge of energy as I awaited its death charge. The creature was going to die, but it was determined to take me with him.

He came at me, jaws wide open. I took a deep breath and dropped below the surface. As he passed over me, I buried the pick into its underside. I felt the water get warmer from all the blood about me. I struggled to the surface and looked all about. Where was the shark?

Then, rising from beneath like a giant demon from the depths of hell, there it was again. Oh, and his eye; somehow there was some vision in his blood filled left eye, and the bastard looked at me with a stare that let me know that this demon was no ordinary shark. This was a hate-filled killing machine determined to destroy me before he, himself, suffered death that he knew was coming. The eye was talking to me, letting me know that death was imminent.

Fall From Apocalypse

Then, I gave the bastard the surprise of his life. I didn't wait for him to charge me. I charged him. What a shock it must have been to him – a human charging a shark.

I met him head on and his teeth ripped into my left shoulder, tearing off more of my jacket than flesh, as I repeatedly jabbed the pick into him. I stabbed and stabbed until my arm became limp, and I dropped the pick.

Bounding free of what he must have thought was a kill crazed human, he made a wide turn about twenty feet away, came to a complete stop, and was trying to locate me. The entire sea was red now, as blood poured out from the numerous wounds I had inflicted on the demon. I couldn't move my right arm, as it was completely cramped from the furious stabbing I had done. I struggled to pull the forty-five out of my shoulder holster with my left hand. I simply did not have the strength to do it. I was totally exhausted from the furious battle. Treading water, I was staring at death.

I was finished, but I was going to battle the son-of-bitch with all I had left. I laid on my back, waiting to kick him with my feet. The shark made one small flip with its fin and belched up everything he had devoured. Parts of Dink were floated on the surface and then were swept away by a wave.

Fall From Apocalypse

The shark was dead. He was dead! Blood continued to squirt out of his lifeless body as he bobbed up and down on the waves. I brushed up against him as I still lay on my back, kicking feverishly to try and make it to shore. Slowly the cramp in my right arm began to subside, and I turned over and started the long swim to shore – the long swim back into B.J.'s arms.

CHAPTER 10
I KNEW WHERE IT WAS

I must have laid exhausted on the beach all morning. Still tired, I somehow managed to pull myself out of the pounding high tide surf and crawl toward some nearby rock formations. Struggling to my feet, I climbed the hillside, found an old dirt road and turned toward what I hoped would be town.

After a couple of hours walking, I came to a gravelled road on my left. I assumed it must lead to town since it was well maintained. Another hour walking and I game to a bluff. I peered down at the town. Easing my way down the hillside, once I got to a asphalt road, an old man driving a truck loaded with junk offered me a ride. It didn't take me long before I realized his biggest piece of junk was the truck he was driving.

I thanked him for the ride and he said in thick French accented English, "where did you come from?"

"The north side of the island." I said as I eased back and took in a few deep breathes.

He grimaced through rotten teeth. "There is nothing on that side of the island, monsieur. Looks like you must have had a really rough time getting ashore."

"Yeah, my boat got grounded on the rocks. I'll have to find someone to come out and help me fix it."

He wasn't buying it. He knew I was lying. "Where would you like me to let you off, monsieur?"

I licked my lips and cleared my throat. "Any hotel will do."

We drove through the outskirts of the town, where dilapidated huts lined the dusty dirt road and masses of black, obviously poverty-stricken people walked about with the typical blank stares of those who were relegated to a life of misery. This was the way of the world now, as capitalism trampled the poor under its jack-booted foot of oppression and used the vast majority as oil to grease the engine of greed.

Another five minutes and it was like a completely different world. Out of the misery and despair into the bright sunshine of wealth and power. Gambling parlours lined the streets and obvious high rollers were strolling down the sidewalks with top dollar broads on their arms. The place was a playground for the rich and well-connected. Like all the rich, they were isolated from the poverty that surrounded them. They could not be bothered. Their only concern was their own welfare and self-aggrandizement.

Fall From Apocalypse

The old guy pulled up in front of a building that looked like the Taj Mahal. I turned to him and said, "you think you could find me a cheaper place?"

He gave me a knowing stare and replied, "I think you should stay here, monsieur. Believe me, this is where you need to be."

I eased my way out, pulled out a slightly wet ten dollar bill and placed it on the passenger seat. I thanked him for his trouble, and he nodded his head.

I entered the hotel and caught the reflection of the old man's truck in the huge glass doors. He made a u-turn at the entrance, parked his truck, rapidly jumped out and ran into a phone booth. What the hell I thought. Maybe he is calling his old lady to tell her he got a ten-spot and they could afford some decent food for a change. For people in his economic predicament, a ten dollar bill was probably a day's wages. Yeah, he'd go to a corporate-owned grocery store that was part of a conglomerate with high salaried executives pulling down millions while the grocery clerks toiled for meagre wages to market the food the corporation forced farmers to sell for less than it cost to produce. Meantime, the corporate marketers doubled the price. Then the distributor doubled the price. Then the grocery store doubled the price. Of course, the farmer at the beginning and the customer at the end got the shaft while the big boys were laughing all the way to the bank.

As I walked through the lobby, people looked at me like I was a freak from some ancient carnival sideshow. Actually, I wasn't sure whether it was the looks or the smell that was attracting the most attention. I didn't really care. I was there on a mission. I was going to take B.J. home, and just maybe, in the process, take out a few organization fat-cats while I did it.

The desk clerk looked at me like he was delighted to have a desk between us. A grimace slowly edged its way onto his face. "Yes sir. Uh, uh, may I help you?"

I grinned as I took the register, swivelled it around toward me and started to sign my name and said, "yeah, you can help me. Make a call to the local police chief and put it through to my room. Then, call a clothing store and order a white shirt, size extra large. Also, order a size 44 long suit, any colour will do. Leg length 34, waist 36. Have them put in a matching tie and socks. Oh yeah, some underwear, large will do. Also, send me up a razor and some shaving cream, a toothbrush and some toothpaste. Just put it on the bill."

He looked considerably nervous when he said, "yes sir. Would you like to pay in advance?"

Fall From Apocalypse

Obviously, he didn't think I was a man of financial means. Wonder what gave him that idea?

I gave him the deep, hard, cold stare. "No, I will not be paying in advance. Mind giving me my key?"

He was too scared to say no. He reached into the mail slot and pulled out a key. "Room 1141."

For an instance, I was a little leery about being up so high. I had always tried to get the lowest floor in hotels ever since reading Wayne Frye's book *Worth*, about the time his dad fell out of the hotel window in St. Louis. Worth had survived in hilarious fashion, but I wasn't so sure that I would be as lucky. What the hell, I was about to go up against a pack of trained killers. Why worry about falling out a hotel window?

As I left the desk, I looked over my shoulder at the still grimacing clerk and said, " don't forget the call to the police chief. It's urgent."

The phone was ringing as I walked through the door. "Yeah, Aaron Adams here."

A coarse, authoritarian, French-accented voice said, "Mr. Adams, this is Chief Arlin. Two of my men will pick you up in one hour. I think we need to see each other and get some things straightened out."

Fall From Apocalypse

He assumed his manner would intimidate me. It didn't. Arlin's name had a familiar ring to it, but I couldn't place it. I took a shower, put on my new clothes and waited. I dozed off for a couple of minutes, but was awakened by a knock at the door.

Two goons in police uniforms stood in the hallway as I opened the door, and they grunted something that sounded like, "let's go."

They whisked me out of town and headed up a mountain road toward a large mansion. They obviously weren't taking me to police headquarters. I leaned forward and tapped the guy on the passenger side on the shoulder, He turned around with his gun in his hand, pointing it between my eyes.

I said, "you always treat tourists like this?"

He obviously wasn't in the mood for frivolity. Without any facial expression at all, he pulled back on the hammer and said, "Adams, we've been expecting you. Every since we got word of the plane hijack in New York, we knew it was only a matter of time until you showed up here. Now the boss would like to talk to you, but I heard too much about you to take any chances. I like living, and even though we were told to bring you in alive, if it comes down to satisfying my bosses or staying alive, take a guess what I'm doing."

Fall From Apocalypse

I liked the guy's reasoning. I gave him the slow, gradual, crooked smile and eased back into the seat without saying a word. I didn't have to. My eyes let him know that I wasn't afraid to die.

An elaborate iron gate brought us to a screeching halt and a guard with an Uzi peeped in to see who we were. He pushed a button and the gate swung open. Hell, this was par for the course. The rich and powerful walled themselves off from the regular people. Even the so-called people's representatives in Washington, DC had to be protected from the citizens they were supposed to represent. There was a time when people could just stroll up to the White House and talk to the President. Not any more, the President was royalty now, and had to be protected from the people. Ditto for the Congressmen and Senators. There had to be a line between the haves and have-nots in society in order to protect the haves from the vast unwashed masses. The organization, corporate executives and politicians – they were all part of the privileged class. However, to me, these people were the leeches of the world who looked with disdain on the working men and women who toiled in obscurity for a crumb from the table of plenty set for the few at the expense of the many.

As we went up the long, winding driveway, I surveyed the area. The walls of the estate weren't that high. I could easily make it over them.

Fall From Apocalypse

There were several cars parked in the wide circular drive in front of the home. We pulled up at the doorsteps and a large man, maybe 6:6 or so and at least 300 pounds, stepped down to open the door.

I eased out nice and slow, but with an arrogant swagger just to let the big-boy know I wasn't intimidated. Obviously, he wasn't impressed. He frisked me, so I rammed my knee into his groin and he crumbled to the ground. The guys in the car came out with their guns cocked and ready.

At about the same time, another guy stepped into the doorway and said, "cool it boys. Cool it. Monsieur Adams doesn't have to submit to a search. We know he packs a forty-five. We have plenty of guns, and he knows we will use them if he doesn't watch his manners. You do realize that don't you Monsieur Adams?"

"I realize a lot of things. For one thing, I know these cops aren't local boys. You import your goons."

He raised his eyebrows in disdain. "Not a very good choice of words, Monsieur Adams. Goon is so distasteful a word for those dedicated to upholding the law. However, you are right, we do import all our policemen from New York, Detroit, Chicago, Kansas City. We recruit only the very best to serve the people of Saint Dominique.

J. Wayne Frye

Fall From Apocalypse

"Yeah, I can attest to their devotion to serving the people. Serving the high and mighty. So, my guess is that you are the Chief-of-Police.

He walked down the stairs, extended his hand and said, "Monsieur Arlin. Yes, I am he."

I recognized the guy. He was some Chief-of-Police. He was Claude Arlin, a Haitian mobster, who had killed his way to the top in the Little Haiti section of Manhattan. He got so hot that the organization decided to whisk him out of town. People thought he had been fitted with some concrete shoes and dumped in the Hudson River. Hell, they had just sent him down to run roughshod over the poor in Saint Dominique. That's the organization. Never let good talent go to waste.

Refusing to shake his hand, I said, "so, I suppose I am here to see somebody more important than you."

"The mayor would like to have a word with you."

As we started up the stairs, I replied, "he interested in getting my vote?"

He looked at me with the contempt of a man who resented someone who did not fear him. "I doubt if he needs your vote, Monsieur Adams."

Fall From Apocalypse

The ostentation of wealth was overwhelming as I gazed down the long hallway that was graced with gold trimmed marble pillars and works of art in little alcoves. About half-way down, we made a left turn into a study that was paneled in luxurious oak. There was a certain bravado and dominance to the room, as if it was supposed to represent the people before me. And the people were definitely men of immense power and wealth. Sitting at the ornate Louis the 15th desk was, no doubt, the mayor. He was a rotund black man of about 50, bald, with a moustache that reminded me of the one worn by Hercoile Pierrot in the Agatha Christie mysteries. To his right was none other than Johnny Mancheko, the number two man in New York's Giancammo crime family. We had known each other for years. To the mayor's left was Abramo Mancini, the Godfather of Jersey City. I didn't know him, but I recognized him from the times he had been featured in TV news programs dealing with crime in Jersey.

Looking down at the mayor, I realized that he was not the real power in the town. The two men standing beside him owned the whole damn place, even the country.

"Monsieur Adams, I am the mayor of this fine little city. I am Marcel Demone."

I starred right through him and panned my head left and then right at his two comrades. Smiling, I said, "you're nothing but a name. These two men are the power here. You and I both know that."

Mancheko let out a light chuckle and Abramo Mancini's eyes betrayed his attempt to stay straight-faced. It was the mayor who spoke up. "Adams, you are not here to insult me. I am in charge here, and I'll appreciate you remembering that."

Mancheko and Mancini remained silent. The mayor pushed a button and three goons with guns drawn walked into the room. Mancheko greeted them with a nod and motioned them toward me.

I went for the forty-five, but it was a waste of time. One of the goons hit me with a rabbit punch to the kidneys, and I crumbled to the floor. The other two men pocketed their weapons, as they kicked me in the ribs. Mancheko stood over me and motioned for them to hold me up. They cuffed their fists under my arms and raised me up.

Mancheko leaned in real close and gave me a rapid one-two to the gut that bent me over in pain. The two goons shoved their fists into my armpits a little tighter, causing more pain as they forced me to straighten up.

Mancheko grinned as he said, "the mayor expects a little more respect, Adams. I suggest you give it to him or things are going to get worse."

Fall From Apocalypse

I was breathing too heavily to answer the bastard, but I did manage enough energy to spit in his face. Mancini moved toward me and pulled his rod. Mancheko motioned for him to stop and said, "hold on Abramo. We don't need him ventilated with lead. I can wipe the spit off, but if he pushes us too far, he is never going to see that good-looking broad of his again, and he knows it. Adams. The mayor wants to talk, so I suggest you listen."

As Mancheko wiped his face, the mayor walked over to me with a satisfied grin. "Monsieur Adams, you have come a long way, and I believe you are interested in finding Mademoiselle Holden. I can arrange that if you are willing to cooperate."

The two goons tightened their grip on me. "I might be interested in an arrangement provided you can produce her."

Mancheko, with an anticipatory air, leaned forward again and said, "then you have the box?"

I had to carry out the bluff. "Sure, I got it."

Mancheko was almost salivating with glee. "Where is it?"

"Where you assholes will never find it unless I get B.J."

Fall From Apocalypse

Mancheko was about ready to piss in his pants with glee. All I cared about was B.J., but I still wondered what was so damn important about the box. What the hell was in it? Mancheko, his eyes lighting up with expectation that he was about to get the damn box, said, "she is nearby. I have her at my villa. It is just three blocks from here. We go out the gate, make a left and three blocks down you walk into her waiting arms. We have people in New York waiting for a phone call. Once the box is in their possession, B.J. is yours."

What an idiot I thought. He just gave me directions to his house. I had no box. So, what was there to negotiate? I would have to figure out a way to get into the villa and rescue B.J. On top of that, the guys were so amateurish they had left my forty-five in the shoulder holster. Sure, they had me in their grip so firmly that I couldn't get to it, but my old friend was still there, just waiting for me to feel its warmth.

I took my right foot, and with the heel of my shoe, gave the goon on my right a kick in the nuts. As he crumbled to the floor, I punched the guy on my left with my suddenly freed right hand. Coming out of their grips so fast startled everyone. As the mayor, Mancheko and Mancini scrambled toward me and screamed for Arlin, who had waited in the hallway, to come in, I dived through an open window into a courtyard. I didn't expect any hot lead to be whizzing toward me, because as long as they believed I had the box, they would only risk killing me if it was a life and death situation for them. I ran like hell toward the pounding surf as a great commotion was going on behind me. I could hear people frantically pursuing me, but I never looked back. Once to the surf, I turned right, because I knew that was the direction to Mancheko's villa, since I was headed in the opposite direction and he had told me to turn left at the gate. I cut up toward the huge homes on the beach. Running between two houses, I made it to the street. I turned left and realized that I had just made it one block. Two more and I would find B.J.

Still not looking back, I reached inside my coat and pulled out the death dealer and turned around, prepared to spit some hot lead from my baby. Apparently, I had lost them at least momentarily. I crossed the street and hid in the bushes around the entrance to a home, gripping the great equalizer firmly in my right hand.

I saw several men emerge from between the houses, and, no doubt, they thought I was continuing down the street. They proceeded toward Mancheko's home. A few residents who were outside gave them a look of bewilderment, but they had no time for explanations. They just continued on their way, thinking they would catch up with me. It was beginning to get dark. I would wait. Yes, I would wait for the cover of darkness.

Fall From Apocalypse

I was careful not to come out of the hedges, but I could see where all the men were turning left two blocks down from me. They were going to be at Mancheko's villa waiting for me. After awhile, I cut behind the houses and walked down the rear alley, until I got to the house across the street from Mancheko's villa. Walking between two houses, I found a spot behind a shrub that shielded me from view.

I waited for the night. Night was my time. The time, when wrapped in the cloak of darkness, I could arise from the depths of hell to deal death and destruction on the blood-sucking bastards who tried to rule with an iron fist. The bastards would fall beneath the scythe, as I, the deadly reaper, on the palest of the four horses of the Apocalypse swept them away one by one. They would all pay for messing with the one thing in life that I loved. And when it was over, B.J. would climb atop the horse with me, and we would scale Mount Apocalypse and stand atop the mountain free, alive and in love.

Mancheko arrived with Arlin and Mancini. They all got out with their rods drawn and surveyed the area. They wouldn't tell one another, but you could see it in their demeanour. The bastards were scared. Hell, they had a right to be. They knew my reputation. They knew I didn't give a damn about my life, and that when I showed I'd have my forty-five cocked and ready to deal death.

Fall From Apocalypse

They went inside, and a guy with a Lugar in his hands came out and walked back and forth in front of the house. They probably had a guy in the back doing the same.

Arlin came out and starting talking to him. He turned his back just long enough for me to move behind some bushes that were nearer the street. I squatted and waited. Arlin went back in and the guy starting walking back and forth again. I saw a dog at the far end of the street. I picked up a rock, and when the guard made a turn I stood up for a split second and heaved the rock at the dog. The dog started barking loudly and the guard ran toward it turning his back long enough for me to scurry across the street and get behind a car in the driveway. I was ready now.

When he returned, I circled around behind him. I tapped him on the shoulder, and when he turned, I slapped his right arm so hard the Lugar fell out of his hand. I kneed him hard in the groin, and as he started to fall, I slammed the butt of my gun against his forehead. He was going for the big sleep. The one that you never wake up from.

Now I was ready to deal with Mancheko. Ready to get B.J. The old instincts die hard. For a split second I was back on the battlefield, back in the mud, crawling toward the enemy. I was prepared to kill, but this time I was not doing it to survive. I was doing it for pleasure. I was going to enjoy it.

J. Wayne Frye

Fall From Apocalypse

In war, you destroy an equal – just another poor slob who is trying to survive in a world that uses those not part of the privileged class as cannon fodder. This was different. These guys were not human beings. They were animals that preyed on the weak and defenceless; human leeches that sucked the life out of people.

I painstakingly, slowly crawled the 200 feet to the side patio in about two minutes. All the way I was reflecting on the times Paul Cross and I had crawled in the mud and slime together. It seemed so long ago in a distant time in a distant war. Yet, maybe it had served a purpose. It had trained me to kill.

Still prone on the ground, I eased up to the patio door. The curtains were closed, but I could hear the muffled conversation. There was a slight breeze blowing, and the curtains parted just a bit. There were five people in the room, and one of them was B.J. She was in a chair near the door. I could only see her back, but that was enough. Soon, I would have her in my arms.

Mancheko was standing near a bar with his hand on top of a phone, as if he was expecting an important call. Arlin and Mancini were sitting on the sofa and a hood, who must have weighed at least three hundred pounds, was actually lying on the floor with his feet propped up on the arm of B.J.'s chair.

Fall From Apocalypse

They all seemed relaxed, as if they were safe with the goons guarding the front and back entrances. Yeah, they were about to find out just how safe they were. What the hell was four more lives in the endless sea of plenty? Yeah, they thought they were safe, but nobody was safe with Aaron Adams on the loose. The bastards had lived long enough anyway. I had them. All I had to do was pull the trigger four times.

I pulled out the 45 and got ready. Just then, the phone rang. Mancheko picked up the receiver, so I decided to listen to what he had to say first.

"Yes, Adams will show up shortly," he said with obvious delight. "We are waiting for him. No doubt the box is still in New York, but we'll get a fix on the location and make sure he and the dame go back to New York with us just to make sure. You finish your job after the box is delivered. You are the one man he fears. After this job, you'll be set for life. You can go back to Mecca and retire."

Mecca! I had sensed it when I saw his reflection. I guess the white socks should have confirmed it for me, but I genuinely thought I had killed him. I was sure I had killed the bastard in a Cairo back alley. Well, that was one I had blown. Apparently, I should have made sure, because he was back to get me. The number one killer money could buy was still on the job. The organization had brought in none other than Magmud El Rausuli.

Fall From Apocalypse

Ten years ago I thought that I had finished him. What the hell, I'd enjoy it. Going up against the best was always exhilarating. However, I had another task that was even more important first. B.J. was waiting. She and I were going back to the city together.

I reached down, picked up a lawn chair and heaved it through the glass door. Rapidly leaping through the door before all the glass had fallen to the floor, I stepped on the chest of the big guy who was lying on the floor with his gun out, guarding B.J. I heard his ribs crack as I buried my right foot deep into him and kicked the gun away with my left foot. I crouched down and rolled onto the floor.

B.J. showed what a pro she was. With her wrists still tied, in all the confusion, she leaned all the way back in the chair, turned it over and cart wheeled out of it, then crawled behind it for cover.

Mancini was the first one to feel the wrath of the forty-five. I tore the top of the son-of-bitch's head off with the first slug, and before Mancini hit the floor, Mancheko caught one in the right shoulder. The force of the blow made him drop his gun and frantically grab his shoulder, trying to stem the flow of blood. Hell, I had hit an artery. The bastard didn't know it, but he was already dead. Too bad I did not have time to enjoy watching him die in excruciating pain.

Arlin, smarter than the other two, did not even try to turn and fire. He headed for the back door in a wild attempt to make it to safety. On the way out, he bumped into the guard who was rushing in the door at the same time. That slowed them both up long enough for me to nail Arlin in the back, and as he was falling, I squeezed off a round that went right through the guard's nose. Meanwhile, as I turned and smiled at B.J., I looked downward and saw Mancheko desperately crawling toward the back of the bar. I fired a bullet into his left arm to slow him down. Hell, I had lost count of how many times I had fired, so I reached in my pocket, pulled out a new round, popped open the cylinder and reloaded.

B.J. was standing there with a sheepish grin on her face. Damn, it was good to see her. She eased over toward me, slid her left arm around my waist, kissed me on the cheek and said, "Tiger, I'm kind of glad to see you."

My eyes told her how I felt. I couldn't utter a word. My tongue just wouldn't move.

All this time, Mancheko was on the floor, whimpering in pain. I was going to enjoy making him suffer like he had made so many others suffer in a life where he dispensed pain like it was an abundant commodity. This time, I was the pain dispenser, and Mancheko would finally get a taste of his own medicine.

Fall From Apocalypse

B.J. interrupted my plan to dispense some pain when she said, "Tiger, we are going to have a hell of a time getting off this island. Not only is the organization here, but Papa Doc Duvalier has troops here as well, and they are here to do the organization's bidding."

"Baby, what we need is some firepower."

Smiling broadly, she offered hope. "Aaron, I saw them unload a cache of weapons and put them in the storage shed out back. These guys are as well equipped as a bunch of mercenaries sent by America to destroy a third world country. Hell, the USA is probably the ones supplying them the weapons to make sure they keep Papa Doc in power." While she was talking, she walked over and picked up the gun Mancheko had dropped. This girl was ready for action.

I stepped over the whimpering Mancheko and poured us a drink. Now I was ready to confront the woman who brought me to the island. "O.K. B.J., now tell me about the box. We both know you are familiar with it."

Mancheko looked up at us with pleading eyes, but we ignored him. Blood was now pouring out of his mouth. He was close to death. B.J. gave me that provocative love you baby look and answered my question with a question. "You know don't you, baby?"

Fall From Apocalypse

"I know that you lied to me about the box. Maybe you have an excuse, but I would like to hear it."

"You should know by now that I used to be a CIA operative. I got tired of all the nefarious, underhanded double dealing all over the world and decided I couldn't take the life any more. That is when I wound up in New York City. Anyway, for years this mysterious box was just a rumour. However, I came across it once when I was on courier duty to Nepal. It's about the size of a cigar box. When I contacted Washington, they told me to get it out at all costs, but not dare open it. I couldn't get it pass customs. There was a tall Arab man standing there with the inspector. The inspector confiscated it, handed it to the Arab and he left. As he was going out the door, I saw him hand it to two white men, turn and go in the opposite direction. I was forced onto the plane, and got a stern going over from my bosses when I got back. I wasn't tortured the way they do it today, but I was kept up for 48 hours and grilled incessantly. They finally decided that I wasn't a double agent and let me go. After that episode, I decided I had enough of the spy life, but I guess I can never fully put it behind me. I contacted them and let them know I might have a lead on the box. It is very important Aaron. Maybe the most important object in the whole world. I don't know why, but it is. If it falls into the wrong hands, it could be catastrophic for this country."

Fall From Apocalypse

"Yeah, and if it falls into this country's hands, it could be catastrophic for the rest of the world. The country you worked for is not all that different from its enemies. In fact, it is a lot worse than some of its enemies. You should not have called the CIA."

She gave me a puzzled look. "You saw me in the phone booth didn't you?"

"Yeah, you'll have to be a bit more discreet next time."

She looked a little hurt. "I'm sorry baby. I guess maybe I have been brainwashed like most Americans. I felt like I had to bring them in on it. Maybe they are bad guys, but they are our bad guys."

I ginned at her. "It's OK, baby. Better Washington than the organization, but there's not a big difference between them. We'll get out of here and get the box when we get back to the city."

"You have it? You really have it, then? I don't believe it. I thought you were just bluffing these guys."

Mancheko began to mumble something about paying any price for the box, if I would just deliver it to the organization.

Fall From Apocalypse

I picked up an expensive bottle of wine. I bent over and bashed him across the forehead. The bastard didn't even pass out.

"Mancheko, I am only going to ask you once. You know what I am capable of, so you better give me the right answer. What the hell does this box have in it that makes it so important?"

The blood had trickled down from his forehead into his eyes. As he tried to wipe it away, he said, "Adams, I swear all I know is that we got orders from the top to get this box. To get it no matter what. Holden was our ace-in-the-hole. We didn't know until we checked with Washington that she had come across it before."

I looked around the bar and found two bottles of Scotch. I slammed the bottles against the bar and poured the contents over Mancheko's blood spattered body. I wasn't a smoker, but I picked up a cigarette from the cigarette case and lit up.

Mancheko looked at me with fear struck eyes. I smiled and flipped the cigarette on his body. The flames engulfed his body, and he let out his last agonizing screams.

As I walked out the door with B.J., I stepped on the big guy's chest just to make sure he was dead. He wasn't, but what the hell, he'd be dead soon. Besides, I didn't have time to bump off everybody who needed killing, but I was doing my damnest to get my share.

I found a car with the keys in it and backed it up to the storage shed. The place was stocked with a variety of weapons. I grabbed machine guns, grenades and even two old fashioned bazookas.

We loaded up the trunk with two machines guns, at least 100 grenades and the bazookas. We headed out of the area.

I was about to deliver a fatal blow to the arrogant bastards who held the island in their iron grip. Papa Doc, himself, would feel the wrath of Aaron Adams all the way back in the Haitian capital, Port-Au-Prince. Washington would be appalled that an ass-kicking independent freedom lover had brought one of their henchmen down a notch or two. Yeah, it would only be a temporary irritant, but it would give me personal satisfaction.

B.J., driving with a determined fury, dutifully followed my directions to the mayor's house. It was 5:00 AM and the lights were all off. I got out, removed one of the bazookas from the trunk, and told B.J. to grab two machine guns. She propped them against the car as instructed and helped me load the bazooka without asking me even once what I was going to do.

"Go to the airport and wait for me in the car."

Fall From Apocalypse

She didn't look too happy, as I grabbed the machine guns and signalled good-bye. She smiled and said, "don't be too long, baby. I don't like waiting."

As she pulled away, I dropped to one knee and mounted the bazooka on my shoulder. The lights came on in the house, and six torpedoes with guns drawn started patrolling the outside as the flames from Mancheko's villa could be seen in the distance. One of the bodyguards passed right in front of the living room behind a shrub. I aimed and fired. He came out from behind the shrub in about ten pieces, as the house went up in a wall of flames. One bodyguard saw me in the street and started spitting lead my way. I caught sight of the mayor as he ran out of the front door behind another bodyguard. I squeezed off another round from the bazooka that nearly put all three of them into orbit.

The four remaining bodyguards, with machine guns drawn, headed down the driveway in my direction. The rat-a-tat-tat started before they were close enough to be accurate. I patiently waited and cut lose just at the right time, felling all of them in one swift sweeping right to left motion.

I loaded the bazooka up once again to deliver the coup-de grace to the burning house, when a police car with a blaring siren came careening up the street. I turned and fired a few rounds in the car.

J. Wayne Frye

Fall From Apocalypse

They slumped over and the car came to a halt as it hit some shrubs beside the driveway. They were both dead. I pulled them from the wreckage, started up the car and headed toward the airport. I made it only a few blocks into town when two police cars pulled across the street, bumper-to-bumper, blocking me. Looking to my left, I saw a department store with a low front window. I turned hard left and rammed through it, coming to a halt in front of the lingerie counter. By the time I opened the door, the four cops were in the store with guns spitting lead. The car door stopped the shots, and I scurried behind the counter. The boys were confused and tried to use a glass counter for cover. I popped up from behind a Playtex girdle and cut loose. Two of them wound up missing the tops of their heads. The other two tried to run, but I stopped one cold in his tracks. A man just couldn't run without his legs. Damn, I loved a machine gun!

The other one made it outside and thought he was safe. Poor fellow, he would never have to think again. I blew the top of his head off.

I walked back into the store and picked up a sexy pair of red panties. The trouble a guy has to got through to get his girl a present. Oh well, it was worth it.

I got into one of the police cars and headed for the airport. Headed to the airport and B.J.

Fall From Apocalypse

I began to laugh and sing at the same time. B.J. and I would be back in New York in a few hours, where there was one more kill I had to make. I still had to tangle with Magmud El Rausuli, and if I lived, B.J. and I would turn that damned box over to the CIA, because I knew where it was now. No doubt about it. I knew where it was.

Fall From Apocalypse

CHAPTER 11
HE KNEW MUCH MORE ABOUT WHAT
WAS HAPPENING THAN
HE SHOULD HAVE

B.J. was not waiting for me outside the airport. I had obviously made a big mistake in sending her ahead. I seriously underestimated the extreme cunning of the Haitian authorities who were linked to the organization. When I strolled toward the terminal, I was greeted by a cadre of armed gendarmes and Tonton Macoutes. I was informed that B.J. had been whisked off to the capital in Port-Au-Prince, where she was the personal guest of Papa Doc himself. There was also a plane waiting for me. Taking the death dealer from me, the captain of the guards escorted me to a plane. Smiling as we sat down, he fondled my friend in his hands as he sat across me, almost daring me to make a move.

The flight to Port-Au-Prince took about 45 minutes. Haiti looked like a beautiful country, but the mask of beauty came off once you saw the people. The ride from the airport to the Presidential Palace in our air-conditioned limousine, shutting out the squalid existence of the poor people who wandered about aimlessly, was an example of the future that awaited an America where the privileged class was rapidly consolidating their hold on the government to effectuate a change that would, like Haiti, capture

J. Wayne Frye   193

the middle class in a downward spiral that would enslave them to corporate theocracy.

The people in both nations were victims of corrupt governments that catered to the wealthy. There was a middle class in both countries, but they were at the mercy of an economic system that kept them all teetering on the brink of disaster. People were forced into submission. In America, the government was more subtle. The populace was constantly bombarded with propaganda that glorified a system based on greed in order to convince people that they, too, could make it to the pinnacle of success, when, in reality, the chances were so slim that most people would be better off rolling dice in Las Vegas. Success was primarily reserved for those who came from success. Those born into wealth inherited positions of power and prestige or had doors opened for them that were only reserved for the privileged. Nepotism was built into both systems. The only difference was that in Haiti, the government was more overt in its control of the people. There were no pretences. Hell, at least in Haiti, the government was more honest – there was no facade of equality.

We were met at the palace steps by an obvious member of the Tonton Macoutes. The dark sunglasses he was wearing in the early morning darkness and his arrogant bearing were a dead give-away. My escort handed him my death dealer, smiled and said, "enjoy your visit Monsieur Adams. I am sure you will find it most pleasant and incredibly enlightening for a man like yourself."

Smiling back with great earnestness, I replied, "fuck you."

The Tonton Macoute goon accompanied me down a long corridor that glittered with gold inlays. I let my mind wander a bit, thinking about the wild tales in regards to Papa Doc keeping zombies in the basement dungeon of the palace. That was just one method to promulgate fear of him among the people. The USA did much the same thing by using fear of communists to keep the American people in line and supporting a system that actually made a mockery out of the word democracy. In Haiti, voodoo was a religion, and it preyed on the weak minds of those who fell for the con games of spells and evil spirits, much as the pompadoured, immaculately attired ministers of mayhem who spewed out hate from America's pulpits on Sunday mornings convinced people that only a stern adherence to their interpretations of righteousness would lead to an eternal life floating on the clouds with Jesus. Otherwise, they would spend eternity in the fires of hell, with the devil shoving a pitchfork up their asses. People were too stupid to realize that the system of government under which they lived had already put them in hell.

Fall From Apocalypse

How could you ever expect people to free themselves from the yoke of oppression when they acted like simpleminded children and refused to think for themselves. It was always easier to let somebody else do your thinking for you. I remembered my friend, Wayne Frye, who once said on the steps of the Lincoln Memorial, "those who refuse to demand their rights, don't deserve any." The world was awash with those who simply lined up for their invisible chains.

I peered out a window and looked at the early morning sun begin to peep over the horizon in the distance. It marked the dawning of another day in the miserable lives of the Haitian people. It was also going to be the dawning of a new day for Papa Doc, because he was about to come face to face with Aaron Adams.

Soon, the sun would be blotted out by the rage of one man. I was a one man killing machine that was about to exact retribution for those poor souls who refused to stand against tyranny in this land of misery.

I was disappointed when a short, stocky grease-ball of a bastard who was dressed like a Prussian general greeted me when I entered the Presidential office. It was not Francois Duvalier.

He had two feathers sticking out of an elaborate sash that cut across his considerable midriff. He strutted about like a giant peacock. What an arrogant bastard. I couldn't wait to pluck his feathers.

"Well, well, you undoubtedly must be Monsieur Adams."

I brought his strutting to a halt with my direct manner. "You know goddamn well who I am you strutting asshole. Now, where the hell is B.J. Holden?"

Both men were taken aback by my disrespectful manner. My escort even pointed my own forty-five at me. The peacock said in a stern manner, "listen Adams, I am the assistant to the president, Clement Bardot. I would suggest you pay me a little more respect."

Remembering some French from my high school days, I replied, "Vous n'êtes rien mais a a amélioré l'escroc qui suce la vie même hors de vos propres personnes pour le gain personnel. Vous êtes l'aisselle de cette nation." (You are nothing but a glorified crook who sucks the very life out of your own people for personal gain. You are the armpit of this nation.)

Obviously, I must have said it correctly, as his eyes nearly popped out of his head and only a wave of his hand kept my escort from slapping me across the face with my own forty-five.

"I'm impressed with your French, but that, nor your crude manner, will get you Mademoiselle Holden."

"What will get her?" I asked, as if I didn't already know.

"You know the answer to that Monsieur Adams. A box, a nice little box that will give me and President Duvalier an inordinate amount of power. We will supply the information to Bumpy Morgan, our agent in New York City, whom I believe you have met. He will, in turn, see to it that we get the box."

Bumpy Morgan, what a cover. The guy who appeared to be nothing more than a low-life owner of a small pool hall in the Bowery was setting up the deal. The guy was connected, big-time. It all came back to me in an instant. The son-of-a-bitch had nearly lit up like a Christmas tree when I mentioned the box. Bumpy knew then that he was about to make the big score by setting me up. I'd have to kill that bastard, too.

I let a note of sincerity creep into my voice. "Well, tell me please. What do I have to do to get my hands on Miss Holden. How are we going to set-up the exchange?"

He got that arrogant demeanour about him again. "Well, Monsieur Adams, that's more like it.

Fall From Apocalypse

A little respect gets you much further than belligerence."

"So, where is B.J.?

As we speak, Mademoiselle Holden is already on her way back to New York on the president's private plane. In fact, she is with an old friend of yours. Well, maybe not a friend, but at least a man with whom you are familiar, a man whom you feared to battle face-to-face, or so I have heard. One whom you feared so much that you shot him in the back. But do not fear any longer, as you do not have to worry about him. We have bought him. He is double crossing the organization, because we are going to set him up for life right here in Haiti or in Saudi Arabia."

Magmud El Rausuli, the pro, I was going to have to go up against the best. Yeah, I was scared, scared that he might kill me before I could get B.J. free of him.

Some what circumspect, I said, "you are telling me that he has crossed the organization? He wouldn't be that stupid."

"My dear Monsieur Adams, it is stupid to bet on a man who is holding a royal flush. The President of Haiti is holding a royal flush. Believe me, my president has much more power than the organization. He is protected by the U.S.

government, and when he gets the box, he will have even more power to use against Washington. They think he is going to help the Central Intelligence Agency get the box, but he will be double crossing them, just like America double crosses countries all over the world. Haiti will become one of the most powerful nations in the world with that little box in its possession."

"You're telling me all I have to do is deliver the box to El Rausuli and Bumpy. Then they will just let B.J. and I walk away?"

"Of course, Monsieur Adams, all we want is the box. You will not have to deliver it in person, just tell us where to pick it up, and this all affair can be successfully concluded. I make a call to New York, and that is the end of it. I assure you we have no further nefarious intentions toward you or Mademoiselle Holden. However, I will tell you that Monsieur Morgan may be a problem for you once you get back. You see, the real Monsieur Morgan has been dead for several weeks. The man you met was, no doubt, very convincing, but he was not Monsieur Morgan. He is a man who has been our North American agent for many years, and is a master of disguise. However, we have no further use of him after we have the box, and he has expressed an unnatural interest in this woman you both call B.J. So, when you get back to New York, you may have to eliminate him. Our attitude is, once we have the box, be our guest."

Fall From Apocalypse

Morgan, why would Morgan be romantically interested in B.J.? It didn't make any sense. Also, it didn't make sense to give them the information on the box while I was still in Haiti. Where was the guarantee that they would release her. El Rausuli hated me. He would love to kill B.J. just to get at me. I couldn't take a chance on doing the deal while I was in Haiti. Yet, I knew these guys were not about to let me leave the country. They were set on doing the deal their way. However, why did I need them now that I knew Bumpy Morgan, or the guy saying he was Bumpy Morgan, was in New York City just waiting to get his hands on the box, so he could deliver it to Duvalier? He would not do anything to B.J., because he wanted two things, her and the box. Hell, I didn't need Clement Bardot. The information he provided me was his death warrant.

OK, I needed to get out of there and commandeer a plane back to New York City. But, how was I going to get my hands on a weapon. The Tonton Macoute goon was still holding my 45, but he was too relaxed. He was making it easy. I leaned forward on my left foot and kicked backward with my right heel, hitting him hard in the groin. He tumbled over, dropping the gun to the floor. Bardot, with no gun, turned to run toward the large golden door behind him. I dived to the floor, picking up the 45 and rolled backwards toward the door to the hallway I had come through, getting to my feet at the same time.

Fall From Apocalypse

I pulled the trigger once, hitting Bardot in the back of the head. Reeling out of the room into the hallway, I ran like a son-of-a-bitch toward the front door, never looking back for fear that the commotion I was hearing might be men gaining on me. I hit the front porch and descended down the stairs, still not looking back. Two guards came at me from the side. I pumped them full of lead.

The alarms were sounding all over the palace grounds, and the army troops about three hundred feet away at the gate to the grounds were rushing up the driveway. No doubt, they were worried that I might have killed Duvalier, himself. I didn't have a chance on foot, so I looked to my right and saw a jeep. The keys were in it. I was on my way.

Bullets were flying all about, and I started hitting bodies as I roared toward the gate at top speed. I hit a guy head-on, and he skidded head first through the windshield into the passenger's seat, all the time holding onto his machine gun. He was barely alive and looked at me with pleading eyes. His legs were still sticking out of the windshield.

I slammed through the gate, spun out into the street and headed in the direction of the airport. The poor bastard who came through the windshield must have been paralysed in the process. The only thing he seemed capable of moving were his eyes. I checked behind me and saw nothing. Obviously, all the confusion was slowing them up in coming after me.

I could see the airport in the distance, but before I got to the main terminal, I had to turn off on a side road to avoid a military convoy of troops that were headed my way. I took the machine gun from the guy and gave it a quick burst to put him out of his misery. He didn't cry out. All he did was die. I knew a lot more were about to die. In fact, I decided that I might just take out the whole damn army and the government along with it. I stopped the jeep, got out and slung the machine gun over my left shoulder, as I made my way across an open field, trying to get to the main terminal when I spotted an F-111 readying for takeoff from the military end of the field. No doubt, it was a gift from the U.S. government that wanted to make sure it kept Duvalier on their side in the insane battle against a communist conspiracy that did not exist. Consequently, as a taxpayer, I figured the plane was partly mine. The only problem was how the hell do you commandeer a fighter jet.

As I was heading in the direction of the plane, the pilot solved the problem for me. He was so shocked to see a fool on the tarmac running toward his plane with a machine gun in his hand that he made the mistake of raising his canopy. Before he could close it, I cut lose with a short burst that went through the side of his face. Hopping up on the wing, I caught a glimpse of a small army convoy heading down the tarmac in my direction. I pulled the pilot out, tossed him on the tarmac and crawled into the cockpit. Having had a few flying lessons when I was only 16, I knew enough to use the throttle to get moving and the rudders to control my direction. The plane roared down the runway. Damn, I was a confused bastard. Guns were firing all around me, and I couldn't figure out how to close the canopy.

Realizing it was futile to try and fly a plane I knew nothing about, I surveyed the cockpit and saw the cannon trigger. I cut lose with a quick burst that obliterated the convoy headed in my direction. The soldiers I did not kill scattered all over the field, running for cover as I continued down the tarmac. Realizing that I had some sidewinder missiles under the wings, I found the button that launched them and cut lose with number one and mowed down a group of soldiers hiding behind some storage bins. The few who survived took off like a flock of wild geese who had just heard a shotgun blast. Maybe I couldn't fly the thing, but I was doing a helluva job with it on the ground. Hell, I was having so much fun I decided to taxi the thing off the runway just as another convoy of armoured vehicles headed my way. I was sky high and ready to leave a message for Papa Doc and his U.S. government backers that they would never forget. When word got back to New York, Bumpy and El Rausuli would know they were dealing with a man who meant business.

Fall From Apocalypse

I was coming for BJ, and I was coming loaded for bear, but first,. I was going to leave my signature all over Papa Doc's Haiti.

I sailed through a wire gate, pressed hard right rudder and swung onto Duvalier Boulevard. After I finished with it, they would rename it Destruction Boulevard. There was almost no traffic on the street, and what there was frantically got out of my way.

An armoured vehicle carrying about fifty solders was coming right at me. It must have been shocking for them to see an F-111 jet aircraft taxiing down the capitol's main street, because the driver come to a halt and immediately threw the vehicle in reverse. However one of the soldiers was smart enough to fire a bazooka round at me that breezed over my head and tore the tail section away. I was afraid he had broken the rudder wire, but somehow, it stayed intact.

The armoured car driver continued in reverse until he got it to a corner and backed onto the sidewalk. Then, coming down the cross street I saw them. Three tanks, one behind the other, turned onto Duvalier Boulevard and prepared to fire. Before they had a chance, I cut lose with a missile that destroyed the middle tank and the explosion made the other two catch fire. Uncle Sam couldn't create a country that provided people with a decent living, a decent education, decent health care or real freedom, but damned if he couldn't turn out some weapons that could create mass destruction. In fact, that was the only thing he was good at. That and making the rich get richer.

When I got to the cross road, I slammed the throttle to 100% of power and hit half right rudder just in time to avoid a well-aimed shot from another tank that would have hit me otherwise. I was at a right angle to them and they had to swivel around to put me back in their sights. One of them never swivelled. I hit it dead centre with a missile, and the force of it slammed the first tank into the second one beside it. They were both burned out cinders in a matter of seconds.

I still had four missiles left. I hit half left rudder and came back to the middle of Duvalier Boulevard. There it was. In front of me was the elaborate, grandiose Presidential Palace, where Duvalier lived a life of splendorous magnificence supported by the U.S. government, while his people starved in the streets. I was about to give the people of Haiti a little justice. I was going to bring down the arrogant symbol of ostentatious living and greed. I just hoped Papa Doc was home. I wanted to fire a missile up his pretentious ass.

I was roaring like a lion on a killing rampage. Between me and the palace was about 500 feet and maybe 500 soldiers. I felt like a king with absolute power. I couldn't see their faces, but the soldiers were obviously scared shitless from the carnage they had already seen me dish out from my road-bound airplane killing machine.

They fanned out and opened up on me with machines guns, small rifle fire and shoulder held bazookas. I cut lose with my cannon and they began to go down like tall grass before a large lawn mower. It was like a man with a machine gun fighting boy scouts with water pistols.

A couple of explosions on the wings and under the fuselage slowed me up, but I just kept the throttle at fill power and ploughed ahead firing the cannon. Within a few seconds, I had wiped out a small army.

There it was, the sun reflecting off the golden dome that sit atop the middle of the rambling palace. This was going to be fun. I just hoped Papa Doc was lounging around with one of his zombies. I cut lose with all four missiles one right after the other. The ground shook as the palace tumbled to the ground with a mighty rumble.

I gave the plane hard right rudder until I made a 180 degree turn and headed back toward the airport. The handful of soldiers who had escaped my earlier rampage were still intent on stopping me. Dumb bastards! A few of them were in front of me, and I never even bothered to fire the cannon, I just mowed them down under the plane. It bounced a little bit as the wheels rolled over body after body. I tried to turn the plane to the right as I neared the airport access road, but there were so many bodies mangled in the wheels and rudder wires that had been exposed from some explosions, that it simply froze up and came to a halt. I grabbed the machine gun, leaped out of the plane and opened up on two guys as they came running down the access road with guns blazing. I got a slight nick on the right arm. Hell, I had made a shambles out of the city, and now I was as hot as a firecracker on the fourth of July. Aaron Adams was a blazing, killing, rampaging, one-man wrecking machine.

I headed toward airport in search of a plane to hijack so I could get back to New York. The blood was pumping through my body like an Oklahoma oil field gusher that had just come in. It had been a long day, and one that Duvalier, the organization and Washington would never forget. And they still had a lot to worry about, because I wasn't through. When I got back to New York, there would be more who would die.

Running rapidly toward the private airplane terminal, I decided to make a turn for the main terminal. Ramming through the main terminal automatic glass doors with a burst of gun fire before they had a chance to open, pandemonium broke out as people started running wildly all about the terminal. Looking behind me, I saw a convoy of troops pull up and come running in. In the mass confusion, I managed to go up the down escalator and get to the mezzanine.

Hell, I was really smart. I always wondered why, in those old movies, a person would run away from a pursuer by climbing up to the top of a building. How dumb, and here I had done the exact same thing. I was worried that I might not make it to B.J. In fact, I decided that this was it, they had me. What could I do?

They would swarm on be like bees to a hive. After I had laid waste to an entire city, and maybe killed at least a thousand people in the process, they finally had me cornered. They would open up on me, and all I could do was fire a few shots back, maybe take a few of them with me, and that would be it.

I was safe for awhile, but all they had to do was clear the airport and toss a grenade on the mezzanine. Hell, they didn't care how many innocent people died. They might not even wait to clear out the airport.

With me dead, the organization would not have the box, but they could sleep better at night, knowing I wasn't out there, waiting for them. Well, they would remember me for a long time, and I wasn't about to go easy.

Fall From Apocalypse

There was no attempt to clear the terminal. All they did was herd all the people over to a far corner. No one could get out, because the army had blocked all exits. Fortunately for the people on the mezzanine, the down escalator had continued running, and they had all scurried down to the main floor. I was on the mezzanine alone.

They probably figured that I would throw my hands up and come out begging for mercy. Stupid, really stupid. What did I have to lose? I was about to disappoint them in a big way.

Aaron Adams was one son-of-a-bitch who knew that we are all born to die, and that there would be no heaven or hell waiting for anybody, only the peace and tranquility of death. What was there to be afraid of? The only regret I would have was not being able to save B.J., but she would know, no matter where she was or who had her, that I died trying to save her.

The army boys were all surprised when I stood up and cut loose with a mighty burst from the machine gun. They simply didn't realize that I was a devil-may-care, ass-kicking son-of-a-bitch who would go down spitting lead.

They were so surprised, at first, they did not even return fire, all they did was dive for cover. The guns rat-a-tat-tat was like a symphony in my ears playing the sweet melody of death. I dropped two soldiers with a burst of fire and the others were scurrying for cover, as I was firing rapidly and moving behind a raised solid metal railing hiding below it and continuing to hold the gun over it, firing blindly.

The people they had herded against the wall broke free and madly ran for the doors. One brave soldier, probably a poor ghetto youth serving the exalted and revered President out of the belief that Duvalier was destined to rule by God's will, tried to hurl a grenade at me. I shot him while it was still in his hand, and a mighty explosion blew him and six of his comrades all over the terminal.

The symphony kept pounding in my ears and the music got louder and louder. I took another clip out of my coat pocket, slammed it in and prepared for what I assumed would be my final assault. Looking at the end of the mezzanine, I decided to make a dash over the wall onto the TWA ticket counter that was right below the mezzanine. I stood up and let loose with a burst of fire. I was just fast enough to avoid the merciless pounding of fire that trailed me to the far wall where I jumped over the landing and came down on top of the TWA counter. I dropped behind the ticket counter and slowly worked my way toward the exit-way. When I was almost to the automatic door, I reached down, picked up a shoe with part of a foot still in it and tossed it on the door pathway to make the door swing open. I was going to make a dash for the runway, and see how far I could get before they cut me down.

Just then, a captain and two sergeants appeared in the doorway, and the nervous soldiers opened up on them before they realized who they were. They hit them with so much firepower that it blew them apart. One of the captain's arms was completely severed and nearly slapped me as it flew behind the counter. I kicked one of the sergeants legs out of the way and prepared to make a dash for life, even if it was for only a brief second. If the U.S. Olympic coach had seen me, I'd have had a place on the team. They opened up on me, but I was so fast, I only got grazed once.

Desperately running down the outside walkway, I saw a guy approaching me who was carrying a parachute. The damn world was coming to an end and this idiot is walking toward the terminal carrying a parachute. He just stood and stared at me. I grabbed his parachute, pushing him down and saying, "gotta blast-off, buddy. Thanks." Hell, a little bit of levity is always good to relieve the pressure.

A small passenger plane was on the tarmac, its pilot desperately trying to get under way and escape the carnage. A guy was just rolling the walkway from the plane, but I slammed the butt of the gun into his stomach and dashed up the walkway before the stewardess could get the door shut. I stood in the doorway too long and caught a bullet in the upper part of my left shoulder. I shoved the machine gun in her gut and ordered her to close the door. She never even batted an eye. She had already seen the shambles I had made out of the terminal, and she knew I was not a man to be trifled with.

My shoulder was bleeding over the nice carpeted floor, and the passengers were all staring at me like I was some creature from the depths of hell come to lay waste to all that stood in my path. Hell, maybe they were right. Maybe I was a creature from hell come to lay waste to all who tried to rule with the iron fist of repression.

Looking about the plane, I could tell instantly that I was on an organization charter. These were all hoods with their wives or girlfriends headed back for New York City. This would be fun!

I made my way forward to the cabin with the stewardess in front of me. The pilots already knew what I wanted, and as soon as I made a motion with my gun, the captain shoved the throttle forward and we went roaring down the taxi-way. He didn't bother to contact the tower. He just took-off from the taxi-way.

Looking at his ADF, I said, "set it for New York City. I got to make an early curtain at a Broadway show tonight.."

He replied, "right. That is where we are heading anyway. Put the gun down, you won't need it."

"It is my friend, I wouldn't feel right with it. So, I'll just hold onto it if you don't mind." I said as I tapped him on the shoulder with the gun and then smashed the radio with the butt of my gun to make sure there would be no communication with anybody.

I made my way back to the passenger section and told the stewardess to get me the first-aid kit and something to eat. All that killing has made me really hungry.

The stewardess was a little on the plump side, but as far as a woman go, she was sure worth a man's time. Too bad I didn't have the time.

"What are you going to do to us?" she said as she was preparing a sandwich.

I smiled. "Worry awhile, baby."

"You're a beast."

"Remember that and you may live."

"I know you. We all know you," she said as she came at me with a knife she had pulled from under the counter. I pulled the trigger and blew her brains out. The other passengers began to scream.

Fall From Apocalypse

One son-of-a-bitch came at me wildly. I shoved the gun in his stomach and gave him the death smile. Hell, he was part of the organization. He deserved no mercy. Maybe he could tell the devil how Aaron Adams blew his guts out with a smile on his face. He dropped to the floor, and I stood there staring at the passengers just to let them know they were dealing with a guy who meant business.

I killed a few gruelling hours tormenting the hoods in the passenger compartment, before I made my way to the cockpit again. As I passed through the aisle with the machine gun by my side, they all looked at me like I wasn't human. Hell, maybe I wasn't. Maybe I was made to kill, to kill all the scum who thought they were part of the entitled class that could lord over the average person. Maybe I was sent to kill those who tried to rule with money and swords. I was perfect for the job, because I could pull the trigger a million times on the scum who looked with disdain on the average man, go home and goet a good night's sleep, feeling no remorse for eliminating those who preyed on the poor, the disenfranchised and the downtrodden.

The pilots were scared. They should have been. "Set your autopilot for Teterboro Airport in New Jersey. And I am no fool. I have taken flying lessons, so I know how to set a heading. Do it now."

Fall From Apocalypse

They did as I requested. I turned to the captain and said, "How long before we are there?"

"About fifteen minutes."

As I headed back toward the passenger compartment, out of the corner of my left eye, I saw the captain surreptitiously reach under his seat. I instantly caught a flash of metal. The stupid son-of-a-bitch was pulling a gun. I pivoted around quickly and let off one quick shot that tore the top of his head off, causing brains to splatter all over the instrument panel. The co-pilot was up and on me so fast that I didn't have time to pull the trigger. We fought for the gun, and I managed to raise the butt-end and hit him in the mouth. As he fell, I hit him so hard on the head with the butt-end that the whole left side of his skull caved in as he fell.

I walked back through the passenger compartment where the supposedly tough guys were all shaking like a bunch of small kids out in a winter storm, wondering what had occurred in the cockpit. They were about to get the fright of their lives, only they didn't know it yet. How I enjoyed bringing down the high and mighty. I picked up the parachute from a seat and put it on.

Since there had only been one shot fired in the cockpit, the poor hapless bastards probably figured one of the pilots was still alive. Still, they

J. Wayne Frye

couldn't be sure, and for some reason, a few of the crazy fools decided to rush me. I opened up with the machine gun and brought their charge to an instant halt.

I walked to the back door, opened it and stood to one side as the force of the oxygenated air rushing out actually pulled the door off its hinges. I will give one guy credit. He had guts. Too bad for him that he did, as I was not a guy it was good to stand up to when I was in a hurry. He spat in my face and said, "fuck you, asshole."

I smiled, grabbed him by the shoulders and pushed him out the doorway. His screams slowly faded away as he fell toward the ground. I looked down at what had to be the Hudson Valley near Teterboro. Right where I wanted to be, I thought. I turned to the remaining deathly frightened passengers and said, "don't worry. I'm just going for help." Then I turned and leaped out the doorway.

The chute opened with a jolt that nearly tore my shoulders off. I slowly descended toward an open field below. It took what seemed like an eternity, but I finally hit the ground. Untangling myself from the chute, I made my way to a nearby house. Fortunately, I did not have to worry about explanations since no one was home. I broke in and made a call to John Havoc and asked him to pick me up.

Fall From Apocalypse

He didn't seem surprised to hear from me, but there was something in his voice that intensely bothered me. I gave him my address, and he took a few seconds to look at a map, came back on the phone and said to meet him at Exit 6 on the New Jersey Toll Way, which was only a short walk from where I was.

I waited by the exit and went back over the events of recent days, thinking how one simple request from an old friend had led to so much death and carnage. Then there was the box – the goddamn box. And, of course, there was El Rausuli. I would still have to deal with him.

The way forward was clearly simple as one scrutinized the intense light of possibilities. Without whim or synonym of reason, there was a mystic allegory of recognizable meaning, a revelation of cause on the cluttered stage of mayhem that resulted from the search for a small box. That cause, my cause, was B.J. My desire for her was a natural miracle. Our united bodies and hearts transcended human bonds, as we became unalterably one in love always and forever. Our hearts and minds were within the twilight of sanctified love that was itself a thread of hope for us in a world that was filled with hopelessness and despair. Together, we were a mighty force that would bow before no incarnation of destructive adversity. Our two wedded hearts could not be stayed by separation, turmoil or pain.

J. Wayne Frye

Fall From Apocalypse

All the way back to the city John was unusually quiet. In fact, there were not even any tirades against me, which was extremely strange for a guy who relished irritating me.

It didn't take long to figure our why he was acting so strange. As we headed down 33rd toward Bumpy's Place, I started recalling certain episodes with him that had bothered me. It suddenly became apparent that over the past few days he knew much more about what was happening than he should have.

CHAPTER 12
THAT DEEP, DARK ABYSS
THAT WAITS FOR US ALL

Night was slowly wrapping its blanket around the city, as John pulled down 33rd toward the Bowery. There was within me a foreboding feeling of something dreadful that was about to occur. The air was hot and humid, even with the air conditioning on. I said, "why 33rd John?"

"You want to go to Bumpy's don't you?"

As we pulled up in front of Bumpy's, it all became crystal clear to me. In the hospital, he had acted concerned for B.J, but he wasn't. He was only afraid that she would die before he got his hands on the box. And then there was Cross and Lawrence. He had been reluctant to furnish me with any info on them. Why? Hell, because it wasn't the organization that took them out. John had done it. He tried to get the box from the two of them, only they decided to go to their graves with the secret. Then, there was the time he picked me up on 7th Avenue. He knew the organization had her then. How? Because he was the contact for Bumpy. He had to be. Then, he had agreed to try and keep Washington out of it. Why? Because he was doing me a favour? Hell no, he knew he couldn't get the box from them, but I was different. I was a friend. It was a contest between John, Washington and the organization to see who got to me first.

I was about to pull the 45, when he quickly reached in his pocket and came out with a 38.

"You know don't you, Aaron?" He said as he leaned against the door, levelling the gun at me. "But it doesn't matter, now. This time, I've outsmarted you, Washington and the organization just long enough. I was on the inside all the time, Aaron. Only trouble was you stumbling in on Alecia at the hotel. That fouled it all up."

I didn't show any fear. I didn't have to. John knew me, and he knew one wrong move and he was dead, even with a thirty-eight in his hands.

"Alecia Cross was in on it?"

"Sure, Aaron. She wasn't Cross's sister. She was a two-dollar whore I put onto Cross. She hooks up with him by offering a little of the sweet stuff. She is there to watch Cross and tell me when the box shows up. Cross got the box, she contacted me, but then you pop in, whisk her off to B.J.'s, and then the organization shows up and really gums up the works.

"What about Bumpy?" I asked.

"Come on, Aaron. You haven't figured that out yet?" He said through a broad grin.

Fall From Apocalypse

The grin did it. Once again, I recalled 7th Avenue the night he picked me up. It wasn't a piece of chocolate on his teeth. It was residue from a tooth cap he wore to block out his teeth and make them look like they were missing.

His grin got wider. "Yeah, you know, don't you?"

"You son-of-a-bitch!"

He couldn't control his laughter. "Yeah, but a damn smart son-of-a-bitch. My acting ain't bad is it? I got the makeup, the false nose, the teeth caps, all from a friend of mine who teaches Theatre Arts at City University. I may take up acting as my new career."

"You'll take up busting rocks in a striped suit when I finish with you."

He was through talking. He made a motion with the gun and told me to get out. He tossed me some keys, and I opened the door to the place. I walked in and there she was, standing next to El Rausuli, who had her by the arm. El Rausuli let her go. She ran to me and wrapped herself in my arms, tears streaming down her face. We were together again, but not for long, unless I figured a way out of the predicament. El Rausuli and John were holding all the cards, and they knew it. Then, I looked in El Rausuli's eyes. He had death burned in them. Hell,

Fall From Apocalypse

I had put that look there. It had been a long time since I had plugged him in the back and left him for dead in that dark Cairo alley, but not long enough to erase his memory. I should have made sure that night. Just pulled the trigger one more time to be certain, but I was young and scared. I wanted to get out before I was discovered. Stupid mistake of an amateur. He was no amateur then or now. This guy was the consummate pro.

John still had the thirty-eight uncompromisingly levelled at me. He told El Rausuli, "get his gun and be careful."

"You don't have to be careful now Havoc. Mr. Adams is only brave when the opposition's back is turned." El Rausuli said as he cautiously removed the death dealer from my shoulder strap.

John looked directly in my eyes. "O.K. Aaron, I want it. No more games. Either I get it, or I turn El Rausuli loose on B.J. I almost think he would rather make you watch him torture her than to get the box. He has a real hard-on for making you suffer some indignities for what you did to him. I never knew you were such a coward. The choice is yours, the box or watch B.J. get tortured by one of the best in the business."

B.J. gripped my left arm with her right hand. "Don't do it, baby. Don't do it. You don't know what will happen if they get hold of that box."

"It doesn't matter, B.J. The organization will get it ultimately anyway. There is no difference between them Washington and John. No matter who gets it, only the few will benefit, just like always. I don't know what the hell is in the box, but it doesn't matter, even if it is a cure for cancer. Somehow, the corporations, the government or the organization will wind up with it. John here is going to sell it to the highest bidder, aren't you John?"

"Already sold my friend. The organization is laying 50 million on me. I'll be splitting it with your friend here. I don't even know what is in the damn box, but I may take a peek before I turn it over to them. I am a bit curious about what I am selling."

I knew what was going to really happen, so I said, "yeah, and once I hand it over to you, we go free, right?"

"Wrong, Aaron. El Rausuli here will kill you, but he will make it nice and quick – no suffering. I promise you that as an old friend. But, B.J, we'll let go. Hell, she may want to leave the country with me and the 25 million I'll have."

B.J. shouted, "I'm fucking going nowhere with you, asshole. And if you know what is good for you, you'll not take that peek into the box. If you do, it'll be the last thing you ever see."

J. Wayne Frye

Fall From Apocalypse

Maybe it was worth a try. It would at least give us some more time. There was no doubt El Rausuli would kill me. He was the kind of guy who would give up 25 million just for revenge. Maybe, just maybe I could buy some time.

I reached in my pocket and threw John my apartment key. Of course, there was no box there. Still, I needed time. I had to come up with a good ruse, because I knew that John would have completely ransacked my place looking for it already. "It's in my bedroom. Take the door to the closet off the hinges, then remove the casement moulding. Behind the moulding, inside the frame you will see an area cut out. The box is inside it. It's standing on its side."

"O.K. Aaron, it better be," he said as he turned and headed out the door, leaving a smiling El Rausuli, who was, no doubt, contemplating the pleasure he would derive from killing me.

Standing there with my forty-five aimed at us, he stared at me, not evening blinking an eye. I figured I had twenty minutes tops before John found out that I had sent him on a wild goose chase. Twenty minutes to figure out how to take out El Rausuli.

"O.K. Adams, the two of you turn around and place your hands on the bar. Keep them there. This time I'll keep your back to me."

I glanced back over my left should and saw El Rausuli sit down on a wooden chair behind a table right near us. He had made a mistake. The table was near enough to allow me to raise my right leg and kick it over with the back of my heel. The edge of the table hit Rausuli's left hand and he dropped the forty-five. But he was a pro. He never stopped thinking. Since the gun was nearer me than him, he realized he was at a disadvantage. He didn't even bother to go for it or the other one he had in his shoulder holster. He just somersaulted backwards, rolled to the entranceway, kicked the door open while he was still on his back, bolted up and ran into the night before I could get my hands on the gun.

As I picked up the gun, B.J. said, "he's gone. He's gone!"

"No baby. He's definitely not gone. He is too smart for that. He's a pro. He'll be waiting outside for us, waiting for us to step out into the night, where he can call the shots. The son-of- a-bitch doesn't take chances. That is why he has been around so long."

There was a note of desperation in her voice as she said, "Aaron, we've got to get to the box before John. We have to hurry."

Very assuredly I replied, "don't worry, baby. The box isn't at my apartment."

"Aaron."

"Listen, I have to flush out El Rausuli."

"No tiger, no." she pleaded.

"B.J., you're the only one who can stop John, now."

"What?"

"Yeah, its been there all the time. We've always had the box. Remember the cigars Lawrence left?"

A light seemed to go on in her head. "Sure, on the top. But underneath, the top layer of cigars is another box. The box!"

"You got it, baby."

"And you realize I will have to give it to Washington?"

"No baby, we give it to nobody. We dispose of it in the Hudson River without ever opening it. Regardless of what happens, you have to promise me that. Washington is no different from anyone else who wants it. I don't know what is in it, but I know that whatever it is that it will not be used for the good of humanity. The rich and powerful would never allow that. They would use it for their own welfare."

"I promise, Aaron. I promise. You are right. That is why I left the CIA. I never saw them do anything good, only serve the interests of the powerful while destroying any hope of social justice in country after country. The Hudson – the Hudson, that's where it belongs.

"Sit tight baby. I'm going to go outside and distract El Rausuli. You get to the office and get rid of that damned box."

"Tiger, I love you."

"That's all I've every wanted," I said as I eased up to the door.

That was it. I was about to climb Apocalypse, about to stand atop the mountain and face the devil. El Rausuli was out there – out there waiting to end it all. I had seven chances to survive. Seven bullets in my 1911 gun. It was the year they put seven chambers in, seven chambers of death. Seven bullets in seven chambers to try and get down from the mountain of death. I ran straight out the door toward some steps going up into a tenement, diving under them surprised that I had drawn no fire. I expected a barrage of hot lead, but I was only greeted with silence. The only noise was the sound of my own laboured breathing. I checked left. Checked right. Left again. Right again. There was nothing. Damn it, where was he? I had to flush him out to give B.J. a chance to flee.

Fall From Apocalypse

I was going to have to expose myself. I rolled over on my left arm, and as I started to raise myself up, a bullet ripped through my right arm slightly below the elbow. The force of the blow knocked me back against the side wall of the steps and I dropped the forty-five. As I struggled to recover it, another slug ripped into my right side, flipping me on my back. I lay there for a few seconds, feeling the life ooze out of me, as I stared at the street lamp overhead. I rolled back over on my stomach and looked across the street at Bumpy's. Standing at the curb was El Rausuli. He had me and he knew he. He just stood there with the gun in his left hand.

Since I had been shot in the right arm, I tried reaching for my gun with my left hand. El Rausuli fired at the forty-five, and it skidded back against the far wall. I had no chance at all. He was going to kill me slow and there was absolutely nothing I could do about it. He was enjoying it.

Well, I wasn't going to die easy. I started to determinedly crawl across the deserted street. If I couldn't get my gun, I'd crawl across the street and start biting on his shoe until I hit meat. I'd take his big toe to hell with me.

Half-way across the street, I struggled to my knees. El Rausuli still hadn't said a word. He didn't have to say anything. It was all written on his face. He wanted me on my knees begging.

J. Wayne Frye 229

Fall From Apocalypse

I summoned every bit of strength I had left and somehow managed to stand up. I stuck my left hand in the gaping hole in my right side to try and stem the flow of blood. It was then that El Rausuli's eyes met mine. We were mortal enemies, but we were two of the best when it came to killing. And at that moment, without one word between us, as El Rausuli extended his left hand and aimed death between my eyes, we respected one another. He had decided to kill me quickly and dispense with the agony I was suffering. This would be the coup-de-grace that ended my life.

Then from behind him stepped the avenging angel. The angel of death wielding a butcher knife that she had, no doubt, procured from the kitchen at Bumpy's place. B.J. plunged the blade into his backbone, and El Rausuli vomited as he pivoted to his right to ward-off the attack. His gun went off. The bullet tore into my right shoulder, and I broke my right wrist as I fell face down on the pavement. I desperately tired to help B.J., tried to force myself off my stomach, but it was no use. My strength was gone.

El Rausuli futilely tried to fight off B.J. She was in front of him now, plunging the blade in and out of his chest. He tried to grab the knife with his right hand. That was a mistake. Two bloodied fingers dropped to the pavement and rolled under me. With B.J. still plunging the blade in and out of

J. Wayne Frye

his chest, he looked at me. He had made up his mind. He was dead, and he knew it. It was no longer important for him to stop B.J. – to kill her. I was the one who counted. I was the one he wanted to take to hell with him.

As he slightly turned in my direction, he fell forward, extended his left hand and pulled off one final shot. The bullet grazed off the pavement and rippled under me. I could feel bits of flesh being ripped away as it skidded along my stomach, came out to tear into my right armpit and shatter bone and flesh as it exited through the top of my shoulder.

Blood rushed up my esophagus, and I vomited as I turned my head to the left to watch B.J. plunge the knife into El Rausuli's back one more time to be sure he was dead. She reached up with her left hand to wipe some of the blood off her face. She looked at me with tears in her eyes. Without getting up, she leaned over El Rausuli's body and started crawling toward me.

"Oh Aaron, oh darling," she cried.

"Don't baby, don't. There is a car in the alley I am sure. Rausuli had to drive here. Check his pocket for the keys. We've got to get to my office."

"No Aaron, I have to get you to a hospital."

"Baby, please don't argue with me now. We have to get the box before John finds out it isn't in my apartment. Don't argue, not now."

She knew she was wasting valuable time arguing with me. So, she gave up, got El Rausuli's keys, pulled his car out of the alley and somehow managed to get me in the backseat.

We were at the office in about twenty minutes. My strength was coming back. What was that old saying about dying - *right before you die, you usually get better for a short time.* Yeah, that was me. I was dying and knew it, but there was one thing left that I had to do. That damn box had to be weighted down and tossed into the river where it could never surface again. I didn't want to know what was in it. Whatever it was had to be evil.

I managed to get to my feet with B.J.'s help. Leaning on her, I got off the elevator. She opened the door and eased me onto the sofa. The office had been gone over with a fine tooth comb, but no one had even thought about looking in the cigar box. There it was – still on the desk.

I looked down at my shoes and they had filled with blood. B.J. frighteningly gazed over at me, opened the cigar box, poured out the cigars on top, then removed another small yellow metal box with a silver rim. Damn, I thought. All this for a little yellow box.

J. Wayne Frye

Fall From Apocalypse

A familiar voice bellowed, "lay the box down on the desk and back away, B.J. Get over there on the sofa with Aaron." John Havoc stood in the doorway with a thirty-eight in his hand.

As B.J. sat down beside me, John moved over to the desk where she had placed the box. "Figured you would be here. Nice job on El Rausuli. Guess I won't be splitting the 50 million now. Maybe I should be thanking you."

He was pleased with himself. "Well, well, this little box certainly has been a lot of trouble to get my hands on, and here it was in your office all the time. Just think about how much trouble could have been avoided and how many lives could have been saved if you had turned it over a little earlier. Perhaps before I collect my money, I should take a little peek to see what I am giving up."

B.J. leaped to her feet. "John, no, don't do it."

I leaned forward, reached up and tried to pull her back down on the sofa, but in the process I only managed to tumble to the floor. She leaned over me, as we both looked up at John. The room became fuzzy, as my consciousness was beginning to fade.

Again, B.J. pleaded with him. "John, I beg you. Don't do it. For God's sake, don't open that damn box."

Fall From Apocalypse

John smiled as he slowly raised the lid on the box and said, "what's wrong B.J., afraid the devil is in here?"

Those were the last words John ever spoke. The whole room begin to change colours. Black, white, orange. Then a kaleidoscopic array of colours seemingly pulsating all about. John's eyes literally popped out of his head, as he looked down into the box. He was suddenly engulfed in flames, and his screams of horror penetrated right through to the very depths of our souls. The whole room was suddenly overwhelmed with raging flames.

B.J. desperately tried to pull me toward the door, as I pleaded with her to leave me and run. Just as we got into the hallway, a mighty explosion ripped through the entire building, and we plunged into that deep, dark abyss that waits for us all.

The End

Fall From Apocalypse

If you enjoyed this book, try these
Aaron Adams adventures from
Fireside Books
(Available from Amazon.com and other retailers)

Armageddon Now
Something Evil in the Darkness at Hopkins House
When Jesus Came to Jersey as the Son of Thunder

And Coming Soon
The Girl Who Stirred Up the Whirlwind

Don't Miss These *Fireside Books*
By
J. Wayne Frye with Jasmine Falling Rain Frye

Points of Rebellion: North American Aboriginals
Who Fought For Justice
Canadian Angeles of Mercy: Nurses in Times of
Peril 1885- 1918
Also by J. Wayne Frye
from
Fireside Books
Called The 21st Century's
To Kill A Mockingbird
by some critics
Hockey Mania and the Mystery
Of Nancy Running Elk